Cole shook his head. "And to think I actually thought I missed you."

"Yeah," she retorted. "I was just thinking the same thing."

He blew out a breath, telling himself it wouldn't do either one of them—or more important, the twins—any good to blow up like this right here in front of the sheriff's office. It was just that he had forgotten just how easily Stacy could set him off. And half the time—like now—she did it without warning. It was like being caught in a blitzkrieg.

"Stacy," he said, growing stern, "let me take the basket in. It's heavy."

"It's not," she argued. Except that it really was. And the babies were moving. With a sigh, she relented. "It's awkward."

"All the more reason for me to take it," Cole told h... For a few brief seconds, she deba...

But her arms were beginning to really ache. So, in the end, she said, "Fine, you can carry them in — but only because I'm thinking of the babies."

TWINS ON THE DOORSTEP

BY
MARIE FERRARELLA

First Published in Great Britain 2017
By Mills & Boon, an imprint of HarperCollins*Publishers*
1 London Bridge Street, London, SE1 9GF

ISBN: 978-0-263-92341-4

23-1017

Our policy is to use papers that are natural, renewable and recyclable products and made from wood grown in sustainable forests. The logging and manufacturing processes conform to the legal environmental regulations of the country of origin.

Printed and bound in Spain
by CPI, Barcelona

Marie Ferrarella is a *USA TODAY* bestselling and RITA® Award–winning author who has written more than two hundred and fifty books for Mills & Boon, some under the name Marie Nicole. Her romances are beloved by fans worldwide. Visit her website, www.marieferrarella.com.

To
Nik and Melany.
Remember never to let
A day go by without saying
"I love you."

Prologue

He was getting too old for this.

A hundred years ago, at twenty-six he would not just have been married but would have had at least three, maybe four, kids. He would have been settled into his life, doing what he could to provide for his wife and children.

Instead, here he was, twenty-six years old and still trying to figure out just what his life would eventually be.

Part of the reason for his surly mood, Cole Mc-Cullough thought as he sat up and dragged his hand through his unruly, shaggy, dark blond hair, was that he was spending two nights a week with his six-foot-two body crammed into a bunk bed. Sometimes three nights. And that was because two—sometimes three—days a week, he worked at the Healing Ranch. The Healing Ranch was a horse ranch run by Jackson and Garrett White Eagle, two of his friends. Their sole focus was to take in and help troubled boys, building up their feelings of self-worth by having them take care of and work with horses.

All in all, it was a noble calling—for the White Eagle brothers. Not that he didn't believe in it. He did. But the Healing Ranch was their calling, their mark in the world.

Just like the family ranch was really Connor's.

Oh, they had all put in their time, he and Cody and Cassidy, but the ranch, left to all of them when their father died, was really Connor's baby. The rest of them had worked on it to show their gratitude to Connor. When their father had died so suddenly, Connor gave up his dream of going to college and became their guardian so that he, Cody and Cassidy wouldn't suddenly find themselves being swallowed up by the county's social services.

He knew that going to college had meant a lot to Connor, but his big brother never hesitated to give it up. For them.

After getting dressed, Cole paused to throw some water on his face in the tiny bathroom just off the equally tiny bedroom. The area had been added onto the main bunkhouse to give him some semblance of privacy. The main bunkhouse was where the boys stayed when their families—and in some cases, social services—sent them to the ranch. The Healing Ranch was a last-ditch effort to straighten them out. Without the ranch, the next stop would have been juvie—and most likely jail.

Initially, there had been only two boys on the ranch. And then there were four. And, as word of the ranch's success spread, there were more. A lot more. Which was why he had wound up working here part-time.

The rest of the time, he was on the ranch, helping Connor.

Always helping.

And while there was nothing wrong with helping his older brother, Cole wasn't building something of his own. Cody and Cassidy had gone on to find their places in life—not to mention that each had someone to share that life with them. Cody was a deputy sheriff and Cassidy was working at the town's only law office and taking classes at night. And Connor was running the family ranch, just the way he wanted to.

Cole sighed. He was the only one of the family at loose ends, not yet sure what ultimate course he wanted his life to take.

Damn it, he was going to be late getting back to the ranch, he upbraided himself. He wasn't going to come to any lasting, earth-shattering decisions by brooding. Besides, this life he was living was a hell of a lot easier than what he and his siblings had been faced with after their father died.

With both parents gone, they'd found themselves close to destitute. Even when their father had been alive, there were times when they had barely gotten by. Mike McCullough would hire out to neighboring ranches on occasion to make sure there was always food on the table. When he was alive, they never went hungry.

Without their father, they found that they had to scramble, doing whatever they could to scrape by.

Miss Joan, the redheaded, tough-talking firecracker of a woman who ran the diner, saw to it that they always had enough to eat. Not one who believed in handouts, she'd made a point of having them work for their supper.

"Work's hard on your hands, but good for your soul," she'd maintained more than once.

So she gave them work. Cassidy had been her youngest waitress to date, Cody did cleanup at the diner, and as for Cole, Miss Joan had him running errands.

Looking back, he was convinced that she hadn't really needed them to do any of those things, but Miss Joan felt that just handing them the money outright wouldn't have done them nearly as much good as having them earn it.

She'd been right, Cole thought now with a smile. Miss Joan had instilled a work ethic in all of them, a desire to make something of themselves.

Maybe that was why he felt so restless. He was still looking for his own niche.

"Not gonna find it here, McCullough, rehashing the same old stuff and keeping Connor waiting. Move," he ordered himself.

There'd be time enough to think about the fact that his life was stalled at the starting gate after today's chores on the family ranch were done.

With that, Cole paused to grab his hat, turned off the light in his bedroom and opened the door. He had his own separate entrance so that he could come and go as he pleased without having to pass through the bunkhouse and all its residents. Two to three days a week he worked with the boys during regular hours and sat with them in the dining hall at mealtime. But Jackson and Garrett recognized the fact that there were times when a man just needed his privacy, even when there was nothing to be private about.

He opened the door and was ready to step out and greet whatever the day held for him.

Or so he thought.

Cole caught himself a second before his foot would have made contact with the wide wicker basket, kicking it and its contents to the side.

Stunned, Cole froze in place, realizing he had come perilously close to all but drop-kicking the two infants who were nestled in the basket, looking up at him with wide, wide blue eyes.

Chapter One

"What the…?"

At the last moment, despite his shock, Cole swallowed the expletive that was about to burst out of his mouth. Given that he had almost stepped on not one but two infants lying in a basket on the doorstep, it would have been understandable, but inappropriate—at least, to his way of thinking.

It took him a moment to come to grips with the situation, not exactly a run-of-the-mill one by a long shot.

"Okay," Cole announced, looking around in the pre-dawn light. "This isn't funny. You just can't leave babies in a basket like this." Getting no response, he raised his voice. "You're not being responsible."

Nobody answered.

Not one to lose his temper in general, he felt himself losing it now. These were babies, not toys or props to be used in a prank.

He tried again.

"Okay, you've had your fun, come out, come out, whoever you are. I've got to get going and babies shouldn't be left outside like this in September. Or any other month of the year, either, for that matter." Again, Cole had to bite back a few choice words meant for the knucklehead who was behind this practical joke.

Cole looked around.

Nobody came out of the shadows.

One of the babies made a sound, catching his attention.

Crouching down, Cole looked at the two infants wedged together in the basket. They appeared blissfully unaware that they were completely out of their element.

"Where's your mama, guys? Or girls," Cole amended. "Sorry, your blankets don't exactly give me a clue what gender you are."

He looked around again, but there was still no one coming out to claim the babies or own up to the rather poor joke.

This didn't make any sense.

With a sigh, Cole picked the basket up and rose to his feet with it.

"Well, you can't stay out here," he said to the infants. "No telling what might come by." Just then, he heard a coyote howling in the distance. "Like that fella. He's probably hungry. Whoever left you here deserves to be taken behind the barn and given a solid thrashing," he said fiercely.

He thought about just walking into the bunkhouse with the babies to demand whose idea of a joke this was, but leaving the infants outside like that was beyond some foolish joke. It was damn dangerous. This didn't really feel like something one of the boys would do.

What if he hadn't come out when he did? Or if he'd decided, just this once, to walk through the bunkhouse to go outside instead of using his own door? There was no telling how long the babies would have remained out here, unprotected.

"Who left you out here like this?" he asked the small faces looking up at him as he made his way to the main house.

"You know, you are awfully cute," he commented to the infants. "Too bad you can't talk and tell me who your mama is, because she needs a serious talking-to. No offense," he added.

One of the infants sounded as if he—or she—was mewling in response.

Reaching the ranch house, Cole realized that he couldn't safely balance the basket and knock on the door so he used his elbow instead. When he didn't get an immediate response, he did it again, harder this time. Because he was jostling the basket and therefore the infants inside of it, he stopped and waited for someone to come to the door.

He was just about to try again when he saw the door finally being opened.

Garrett White Eagle was not usually at a loss for words but this was one of those few times when his mind seemed to go blank.

Recovering, Garrett opened the door to the main house wider and asked Cole, "Have you taken up selling babies door-to-door? Because I'm pretty sure that your brother Cody will tell you that's illegal."

Perturbed, Cole didn't bother commenting on Garrett's assessment. Instead, he told the man, "I almost tripped over these two when I was leaving this morning. Some brainless jackass left them on my doorstep."

"Cute little things," Garrett observed. "Bring them into the living room."

He gestured into the house, then led the way to where he, his brother and their wives gathered in the evening, usually with at least a few of the boys who were making progress in the program.

Cole placed the basket on the wide, scarred coffee table just as Garrett called out toward the kitchen, "Hey, Jackson, could you come in here? You've just got to see this."

A minute and a half later Jackson White Eagle, taller and slightly more muscular than his younger brother, walked into the living room.

"What's all the commotion abou—" Jackson stopped dead in his tracks. His eyes went straight to the basket on the coffee table. "Garrett, what are two babies in a basket doing on our coffee table?"

"Don't look at me," Garrett protested. "They belong to Cole."

"Cole?" Jackson asked incredulously. His eyes shifted to the cowboy he'd hired to work part-time on their ranch.

"No, they don't," Cole denied with feeling. "I just stumbled over them on the doorstep as I was leaving this morning."

"*Your* doorstep," Garrett pointed out, obviously thinking that was the key word.

Cole shook his head, trying to distance himself from any responsibility. "I'm beginning to think that was just a mistake."

"*Your* mistake?" Garrett asked, eyeing his friend closely. "Did you get some ladylove in the family way, Cole?"

Garrett sat down on the old brown-leather sofa in front of the babies. He made a few cooing noises at the infants, which seemed to entertain them sufficiently to get them to stop whimpering.

"Forever is just a little larger than a postage stamp," Cole pointed out, referring to the nearby town. "I think if something like that had happened, *everyone* in Forever would have known—if not immediately, then soon enough."

"So, these little cuties aren't yours?" Garrett asked, just to make sure.

If they had been his, Cole would have owned up to it without any hesitation and done the right thing by the babies' mother. Cole felt that his friend knew him well enough to know that.

Cole frowned at Garrett. "No."

"You're sure about that?" Jackson asked, looking at Cole closely.

"Absolutely," Cole answered, but just the slightest note of hesitation had entered his voice.

What if…?

No, no way. It wasn't possible.

The only woman he'd been intimate with in the last year had been Stacy Rowe. But Stacy had suddenly taken off not too long after that, leaving without a single word to him. Leaving as if the evening they had spent together had filled her with regrets.

Or maybe, according to the rumor he'd heard later, her Aunt Kate had insisted Stacy come with her on "the vacation of a lifetime," then whisked her off on a prolonged tour of Europe.

Having her leave like that, without warning, had really hurt him, although he'd said nothing to anyone, not even his family. He'd thought that he and Stacy had something unique going, but obviously she hadn't shared his feelings.

In time, he got over it.

Or so he told himself.

"Well," Jackson was saying, turning to look at him. "What are you going to do with them?"

Cole looked at the other man, stunned. "Me?"

"Well, yes," Jackson replied. "They were left on your doorstep."

Cole still doubted that had been the person's actual intention. He didn't always stay over the same days. He could just as likely have *not* been here. "Undoubtedly by mistake."

"Maybe not," Jackson said thoughtfully.

"What are you talking about?" Cole asked.

"Your brother Cody came to his future wife's rescue and wound up delivering a baby," Jackson reminded him. "And didn't Cassidy rescue that baby from the river not too long after that?"

"Yes," Cole answered cautiously, not sure where Jackson was going with this.

"Can't be a coincidence," Jackson told him. "Somebody probably feels that your family's good with babies. Want my suggestion?" Before Cole could say anything in response, Jackson told him, "Take the babies home with you until you can sort this whole thing out."

"Wait," Cole said, feeling as if this whole thing was just spinning out of control. "You're forgetting one important thing. You've got a ranch full of teenage boys, all of them old enough to father a child—or two," he pointed out.

Jackson studied the infants for a moment. "My guess is that these babies are about three or four weeks old. Maybe less."

"Okay," Cole said, waiting for Jackson to make a point.

"That means that if they were fathered by one of the boys on the ranch, it would have had to have happened about ten months or so ago," Jackson told him.

"Right," Cole agreed, still waiting for Jackson's point.

"Well, we've only got three boys who have been here that long," Jackson concluded. "The rest have been here for less time than that." There were several who had graduated the program and returned home in that time frame, but for now, he decided not to mention that. He still felt that the infants might be Cole's.

"Okay!" Cole was on his feet. "Let's go talk to those three hands."

The babies were making more noise. Jackson's attention shifted to them. "Well, before we do that, I think these two little people need to be fed first."

Feeling suddenly, totally, out of his depth, Cole looked around.

"Is Debi here?" Jackson's wife, Debi, was a registered nurse who worked at the town's only medical clinic.

Jackson shook his head. "She went in early today. It's her turn to open the clinic."

"What about Kim?" Cole asked hopefully, looking at Garrett.

"Sorry, out of luck there," Garrett told him. "Kim's away on assignment. She left last week. She still keeps her hand in," he explained proudly, "doing occasional stories for the magazine that brought her out here in the first place."

Obviously taking pity on Cole, Jackson volunteered, "However, Rosa's here," referring to the Healing Ranch's resident housekeeper.

Cole was immediately hopeful. "Do you think that she could...?"

"She might, if we ask her nicely," Jackson speculated.

"She's probably in the kitchen. I'll go get her," Garrett volunteered, taking off.

The babies were beginning to fuss in earnest now.

Cole looked at Jackson. "You don't think that these belong to one of those boys you mentioned, do you?"

"Highly doubtful," Jackson said. Moving toward the basket, he picked up the louder of the two infants and began rocking it in an attempt to quiet the baby. "You've seen the hands. By the end of the day, they're all too tired to chew, much less try to romance some little lady. Besides, so far this is still an all-male program we have going here. To find a girl his age, our Romeo would have to ride all the way out to town or the reservation. I'd probably know about it if that happened," Jackson assured him.

"Where did these babies come from?" Rosa Sanchez asked as she walked into the living room.

"That's what we're trying to find out," Jackson told the woman.

Maternal instincts rose to the surface. Rosa picked up the other infant from the basket and held it against her ample bosom.

"Oh, the poor little thing," she cooed. "He is hungry."

Cole stared at her, surprised. "You can tell it's a he? How?" he asked, then pointed out, "The baby's all bundled up. They both are."

Rosa merely smiled. "He is noisier. Men usually are," Rosa told him knowingly. She looked at Jackson. "Bring the other one," she instructed the man who was technically her boss. And then she turned toward Cole. "You bring the basket. There is no place to lay them down while I take turns feeding them, so the basket will do."

"Rosa, how are you going to feed them? We don't have any baby bottles," Garrett asked.

"Boil a cloth," Rosa instructed Jackson.

He looked at her in confusion. "And just how is that going to…?"

"When it is clean, we will dip a corner of the cloth into a cup of warm milk and the baby will suck on that."

"Won't that take a long time, feeding him that way?" Cole asked.

Rosa gave him what passed for a patient smile. "Just until one of you comes back from the general store in town with two baby bottles," she replied. "Now go, go," she urged them. "These babies are getting hungrier by the minute."

"I'll go to the general store," Garrett volunteered, no doubt thinking that was the safest thing for him to do.

"I'll make breakfast for the boys," Jackson told his housekeeper, handing off the baby he'd been holding to Cole. "You stay here with Cole and the babies, and do what needs to be done."

Rosa smiled at him patiently. "Yes, Mr. Jackson."

THE PROCEDURE WAS slow and tedious, but, to Cole's surprise, feeding the infants Rosa's way seemed to satisfy them, at least for the time being.

"I think this one's going to suck in the cloth," he marveled, watching the infant in his arms going at the milk-soaked cloth he was bringing to its lips.

"Don't forget to keep soaking the cloth," Rosa prompted. "You don't want it getting dry."

"Right," Cole murmured, taking the cloth he had wrapped around his index finger away from the infant's mouth and dipping it into the milk he had standing in one of the coffee mugs.

"Mr. McCullough?" Rosa said.

Cole raised his eyes away from the infant he was attempting to feed. It was touch and go at the moment. "Yes?"

"You are sure you are not the father of these babies?" she asked in a low voice. Before he could say anything, she assured him, "It is just the two of us here right now. You can tell me." She leaned her head in toward him and said in a low voice, "I will not tell anyone."

"I'm sure, Rosa," Cole said patiently.

And, for the most part, he was. There was just this tiny little inkling of doubt left, but he knew he was needlessly torturing himself. If there had been a baby— or babies—because of that one wondrous night, Stacy would have told him.

Wouldn't she?

"Then why would someone leave them on *your* doorstep?" Rosa asked, dipping the edge of her cloth in the warm milk. "Why not with the sheriff or on the clinic's doorstep?"

"I really don't know, Rosa." The next moment, he exclaimed, "Wow! I sure am glad this baby doesn't have teeth yet. He's got really strong lips for an infant."

He carefully maneuvered his finger out of what appeared to be a steely rosebud mouth.

"She," Rosa corrected.

He looked at the housekeeper, confused. "She?"

Rosa nodded her head.

He gazed at the infant. She was all bundled up in yellow. Both of the babies were. Yellow was neutral. It didn't indicate either male or female. "How would you know that?"

Rosa smiled. "I have a gift," she told him calmly.

His eyes narrowed just a little. "You unwrapped this one, didn't you?"

The corner of Rosa's eyes crinkled just a little more as she laughed. "Perhaps I did, a bit," she admitted.

Rosa's laugh was infectious and Cole caught himself laughing, as well. Doing so made him feel just a little better—at least, for now.

Chapter Two

Stacy Rowe was amazed.

She'd been born and raised in Forever, and a little more than eight months ago she would have said that it felt as if things never changed in this tiny town. And then Aunt Kate had whisked her away on that European vacation—insisted on it, really—saying that she wanted Stacy to open her eyes and see that there was a world beyond Forever.

And, more importantly, a world beyond Cole McCullough.

The second his name flashed across her mind, Stacy clenched her fists at her sides as if that would somehow chase away any and all thoughts of the tall Texan.

She wasn't ready to think about Cole yet.

Cole was the reason that she'd left Forever eight months ago.

And he was the reason she almost hadn't come back. She didn't want to see him, not yet.

Maybe not ever.

Not after what had happened.

But she really didn't have that much choice in the

matter. Aunt Kate, that unbelievably hearty, dynamo of a woman, had suddenly become ill in Venice. Never one to complain, Aunt Kate had waved away all of Stacy's voiced concerns—right up to the time she'd taken a turn for the worse and died before a flight home could be hastily arranged.

Aunt Kate's death had complicated matters far beyond the immediate emotional component. Alone in a foreign country, Stacy had felt utterly stranded. Aunt Kate had always insisted on handling everything and it was easier than arguing with the woman, so she had let Aunt Kate do it.

It had taken every fiber of her being for Stacy to rally, pull herself together and do what needed to be done.

Per her aunt's specified last wishes, she'd had her aunt's body cremated and then she'd flown back to Forever with an urn filled with Aunt Kate's ashes.

Stacy would rather have flown anywhere else, but in all honesty, she couldn't afford to travel any longer or go anywhere except the town she'd always called home. Aunt Kate had been the one with all the money.

Her aunt had left her a little money in her will, but that, too, required a trip back to Forever. Olivia Santiago, along with her partner, Cash Taylor, ran the only law firm there. As Aunt Kate's attorney and executor, Olivia had the only copy of her aunt's will.

So, with a heavy heart and more than a little reluctance, Stacy had returned. Once back, she'd presented Olivia with a copy of her aunt's death certificate.

And that was when she discovered that some things in Forever *had* changed. The house that she'd grown up in, the one that her mother had left to her when she died and where she and Aunt Kate had lived before they'd gone off to Europe, had burned down while they'd been away.

The other thing that had changed while she'd been gone was that Forever had finally gotten its first hotel up and running. What that meant was that at least she had a place to stay while she waited for Olivia to square things away for her when it came to the will.

This was her first week back and, hopefully, her last.

Getting up, Stacy got ready quickly, intending to go downstairs to get some much-needed coffee and eggs over easy. The hotel, still in its infancy, had just opened a small restaurant on its premises. She'd heard it was having some trouble with a faulty refrigerator, but supposedly that had been taken care of. She crossed her fingers.

Stacy got off the elevator and was crossing the lobby to get to the restaurant when she heard Elsie, the young woman behind the reception desk, let out a loud, blood-curdling scream.

Hurrying over, Stacy put a comforting hand on the young girl's shoulder and asked, "What's wrong, Elsie? Can I help?"

Elsie didn't appear to hear her or even be overly aware that anyone was standing next to her. Her attention was completely centered on the paper she was clutching.

"I did it!" Elsie cried, waving what looked like a letter in her hand. "I did it! I'm going to college!" she squealed.

Scurrying out from behind the desk, she threw her arms around Stacy, and then around Rebecca Ortiz, the hotel manager who had been drawn out of her office by the noise. "I'm going to college!" Elsie repeated, obviously beside herself with joy.

"Somewhere not too far away?" Rebecca asked, obviously doing her best to share the moment with the receptionist.

Elsie stopped abruptly and then happily grinned at the manager. "I'm going to be going to the University of Texas in Austin," she told her small audience proudly.

"Oh. That means you'll be going away to school."

"Yes, it will," Elsie cried happily, her eyes all but dancing as she moved around the lobby. "And I can't wait to go."

"Well, you've still got some time," Rebecca pointed out. From her expression, she was already trying to figure out how to get a replacement for Elsie. "You just came back from an extended vacation. And next September's a long way away."

Elsie shook her head so hard it looked as if it was going to go spinning off. The young girl held the letter up higher.

"No, it says here I can start in January, just like I applied." The girl's eyes were dancing. "There are so many things I have to do! I can't wait to call my parents and tell them about this!"

"You didn't tell them when you opened the letter?" Stacy asked.

With all her heart, she wished she had parents she could share things with. With Aunt Kate gone, she was on her own.

"I, um, didn't open the letter when I got it," Elsie confessed, sounding just a little subdued for a moment, like she was tripping over her words. "I've been carrying it around since yesterday. I was afraid that the school had rejected me. But they didn't!" she exclaimed, her voice rising again. "They said yes!"

"Yes, we know, dear." Rebecca sighed. "Looks like I'm going to have to find a new receptionist for the hotel. Quickly," she added.

Turning toward Stacy, she ventured, "You wouldn't be looking for a job, would you?"

"Well, if it'll help you out—" Stacy began, gauging her words slowly.

Rebecca's eyes widened in surprise. "Oh, it would, it definitely would," she assured Stacy. "I realize that you probably won't be staying permanently, but I'd really appreciate you taking over for Elsie when she leaves." As an afterthought, Rebecca turned toward the receptionist and asked, "When are you planning on leaving, dear?"

"This minute!" Elsie all but shouted. It was like watching champagne bubbling out of a bottle a moment after the cork had been pulled. "I've got so much to do between now and January." Moving from foot to foot, the now former receptionist gave the impression that she was about to jump out of her skin at any second.

"Things are finally turning around and going my way," she cried. "I've got to get home. I've got to tell Mom and Dad I'm going to college." She paused for a split second before charging out the front door. "I'm going to college!" she cried, as if she couldn't get enough of the simple declaration.

And the next moment, she was gone.

Rebecca shook her head and laughed. "Can you remember ever being that excited?" she marveled, glancing in Stacy's direction.

"Once, a lifetime ago."

At least, it felt like a lifetime ago. But in reality, it wasn't. She'd been that happy when she'd found herself falling hopelessly in love with Cole McCullough. In the beginning she'd been convinced that it was strictly one-sided—until he began paying attention to her.

She remembered every word of every conversation they'd ever had. Cherished all the islands of time that they'd shared together. Back then—had it really been less than a year ago?—she'd honestly believed that maybe, just maybe, they were on their way to meaning something to one another.

Oh, Cole had meant a great deal to her, he had for years now, but it wasn't until they started spending time together that she began to believe that maybe, just maybe, there was a happily-ever-after in store for her. For *them*.

She should have realized that she was too old to believe in fairy tales, Stacy admonished herself. They'd had one wonderful, magical night together, and then he'd turned around and told her that maybe things were moving too quickly. That they should slow down before it was too late.

As far as she was concerned, it was already too late. Like a lovestruck idiot, she'd thought he felt the same way about her that she did about him. She should have known better.

She'd given Cole her heart and he had stomped on the gift, offering her a bunch of meaningless rhetoric that, loosely interpreted, said *I had a great time. Don't let the door hit you on the way out.*

She'd always been the smart one in her family; at least, that was what Aunt Kate had always told her. But Aunt Kate found her crying in her room. Stacy had tried to pretend that nothing was wrong, but her aunt hadn't been fooled. Then Kate put two and two together, and just like that, the idea for the European vacation had been born.

Stacy had attempted to demur, but Aunt Kate wouldn't take no for an answer. She'd said that she always wanted to travel abroad and felt that this might be her last chance.

Little did either one of them realize that she would be right, Stacy thought sadly.

In hindsight, Stacy didn't regret taking off the way she had. Hurt, she hadn't thought that she owed Cole a single word of explanation, or even the courtesy of a goodbye since he had distanced himself from her right after their night together.

And, looking back, she was glad she'd had that time with her aunt.

What was hard was finding a place for herself now that she was back.

Well, that wouldn't be a problem for the time being. Thank heavens she'd been in the right place at the right time. Any possible future money problems, at least for now, were on hold.

"When would you like to get started?" Rebecca asked her.

Stacy shrugged. She hadn't even been thinking about this half an hour ago.

"Now would be fine," she finally told the hotel manager.

"Now?" Rebecca echoed, surprised. "You don't want a day to wind down and get used to the idea?"

Stacy saw no advantage in that. At least if she was working, she'd be doing something to occupy her mind, although she had to admit it didn't exactly look extremely busy around here.

"Why?"

The question took the hotel manager aback. "Well, when you walked into the lobby this morning, I *know* you weren't thinking about being able to get a job as a receptionist."

Stacy laughed.

"I wasn't *not* thinking about it, either."

Pleased, Rebecca put her arm around Stacy's shoulders and gave her a quick squeeze. "I do appreciate this, Stacy. It saves me the trouble of having to look for someone to take Elsie's place. You are a lifesaver. You know that, don't you?"

"It goes both ways, Rebecca." When the taller woman looked at her quizzically, Stacy decided not to tell her that she needed a job or would need one eventually. Instead, what she said was, "I need to keep busy."

"Well, we don't exactly have so much business that we have to turn people away," Rebecca told her honestly. "This *is* still Forever. But slowly we are getting outsiders passing through, especially ever since the Healing Ranch was written up in that magazine. That put us on the map, so to speak. Before then, except for the occasional lost person who found themselves in Forever by accident, looking for the right way to get back, I don't think anyone ever came to Forever on purpose. Not unless they already lived in the general area and were just coming into town for supplies."

Rebecca was not telling Stacy anything that she didn't already know.

"All things considered," Stacy said honestly, "I'm kind of surprised that someone actually built a hotel in Forever."

Rebecca smiled. "Just between us…me, too," she told Stacy with a broad wink. "There's not much to this job, really," she went on. "I can train you in an hour. Half that time if you're as smart as I remember."

They'd attended the same high school together— everyone in Forever did—where Rebecca had been three years ahead of her. But since the classes at each grade level were rather small, it felt as if the students were more like one large family than the typical rivalry between the different grades.

Stacy blushed a little. Compliments were a rare thing in her world. Not that Aunt Kate had been belittling. She just had a way of taking everything over, silently indicating that she didn't feel that her niece was competent to do things as well as she herself could do them. For a while there, Stacy had begun to believe her.

"You're being kind," Stacy responded.

"I'm being accurate," Rebecca corrected. "Remember, I'm your boss for now. Bosses don't get anywhere by being just kind. They have to be accurate. I think you're going to be good for the hotel.

"Okay, let me go over some of the key duties, and then you can get started by going to the diner and getting some breakfast for the two of us."

Stacy looked at her, curious. "I thought the hotel had that little restaurant on the premises." She recalled walking by it yesterday.

"It does," Rebecca told her. "But unfortunately, it's still closed for repairs."

"Repairs?"

The other woman nodded. "It seems that yesterday, just before end of day, we had a grease fire. There was some damage done. We're keeping it closed for now. Just one thing after another," she said with a sigh. "You don't mind going, do you?" she asked after seeing the slightly unhappy expression on Stacy's face.

"Oh, no, no problem."

Which was a lie. She hadn't ventured out to see anyone except for Olivia since she'd returned.

But she knew that she'd have to face people eventually and field questions. There was no such thing as "mind your own business" in Forever. But she had really thought that *eventually* wasn't going to arrive so soon.

Obviously, she'd thought wrong.

So, after a very brief review of her new duties, which, Stacy felt, anyone with an ounce of common sense could have easily figured out, she found herself walking to Miss Joan's Diner.

She knew she could have driven there, giving herself a quick avenue of escape once she'd placed and picked up her order, but that was only putting off the inevitable. She had to face the people of Forever who would have questions for her.

It was better to get it over with than to stress over the anticipation of what those questions might be.

You can do this, you can do this, Stacy told herself over and over again, like some sort of a mantra meant to give her strength as she made her way down the streets of Forever to the diner.

You can do this. You can do this.

Finally reaching the diner's front door, she pulled it open and walked inside. Several people at the counter looked up in her direction. She saw recognition ricochet back and forth on their faces.

You can't do this.

Chapter Three

The babies had both been fed and, thanks to the resourcefulness of Jackson and Garrett's housekeeper, they had been changed as well, so their whimpering, at least for now, had stopped. The twins had fallen asleep.

Cole took the opportunity to call home. It took several rings before anyone picked up on the other end.

"Hello?"

Cole could tell by the way the greeting had been barked that Connor was in less than good spirits. "Connor, it's Cole. I'm going to be late."

"You're already late," his older brother informed him.

"I know," Cole said, an apology implied in his voice. "But it can't be helped."

"*Everything* can be helped," Connor said impatiently. And then Cole heard his older brother sigh. "Okay, well, what's the problem?"

Looking at the sleeping twins, Cole moved farther away from them, afraid that if he accidentally spoke loudly he'd wind up waking them up. "You know how

Cody came across Devon pulled over on the side of the road and she was about to give birth?"

"Yes?" Connor sounded perplexed.

"And then Cassidy helped save that baby out of the river?"

"I've got chores to do, Cole. For both of us, it appears. I know all this you're telling me. What I don't know is where you're going with it."

Cole took a deep breath. "Well, it seems that it happened again."

"*What* happened again?" Cole sounded as if he was coming to the end of his patience.

"I was about to leave the ranch when I found these two babies on the doorstep."

"Two babies," Connor repeated incredulously.

"Yeah. They're twins."

Connor sighed. "Of course they are. Whose are they?" he asked.

"Haven't a clue," Cole admitted. "They were just there, tucked into this huge wicker basket like laundry—breathing, moving laundry."

There was a long pause on the other end of the line and then Connor finally began to ask, "Cole, did you by any chance, um…"

Cole knew what was coming and immediately headed it off before Connor had the opportunity to finish the sentence. "No, I didn't, Connor. Those babies are not mine."

"I'm just going to ask this once, and then we'll

put this to rest," Connor promised before he pressed, "You're sure?"

"I am positive," Cole said with finality.

There was no mistaking the relief in Connor's voice. "Okay. Then you've got to find out who those babies belong to."

"I know," Cole answered. "I'm taking them into town to see if anyone there knows anything. I'm sorry about this."

Connor's voice took on his customary understanding tone. "Don't be. This isn't your fault. Give me a call when you find out who abandoned them like unwanted puppies."

"The second I find out," Cole promised just before he terminated the call.

Returning to the living room, where Rosa was sitting next to the sleeping infants, Cole began to pick up the basket.

Rosa stopped him with a look. "Where are you going?" she asked.

"I'm taking them into town to see if anyone there knows who these little guys really belong to."

"Only one of them is a little guy," Rosa reminded him.

Rosa had been right. One of the twins was a girl.

"I know," Cole answered. With that, he walked toward the front door with the basket in his hands.

Rosa was on her feet and wound up beating him to the front door. Her agility was rather impressive for a woman her age. "You cannot put them on the seat next to you in the truck," she warned.

He smiled at this protective side of the woman. "I don't intend to, Rosa. Don't worry," he told her. "They'll be safe."

"Safe" involved some clever work with the wicker basket and a length of strong rope. Securing the latter around the former, then tying the basket to the seat, Cole was able to drive into town.

Forever had a medical clinic as well as a sheriff's office, but there was no question in Cole's mind what his first stop with the twins was going to be.

He drove straight to Miss Joan's Diner.

If anyone would have a clue as to who the twins' mother was, it would be Miss Joan. Like most of the town's other citizens, Cole was of the opinion that nothing happened in Forever and its outlying territory without Miss Joan knowing about it. Half fairy godmother, half hard-as-nails taskmaster, Miss Joan seemed to know everything about everyone.

And, if she didn't know now, she would before the end of the day. No one doubted that the woman had her finger on the pulse of the entire town.

Cole himself had an exceedingly soft spot in his heart for the woman. Miss Joan had been there for him and for his siblings when their dad died, and although she could be blustery and demanding, and had been on more than one occasion, he knew that beneath all the tough talk, Miss Joan had the proverbial heart of gold. Even though she would be the first to deny it.

However, that didn't change anything.

Cole parked his truck right in front of the diner. His vehicle was blocking the entrance to some degree, but he thought that, just this once, given the circumstances, he'd be forgiven.

Undoing the ropes that were holding the basket and its precious cargo in place, he picked up the twins and made his way into the diner.

The moment he walked in, Cole knew he had Miss Joan's full attention, even though she was behind the counter and on the far side of the diner.

A couple of the waitresses, Eva and Rachel, reached him first, oohing and aahing over the infants in the basket.

But it was Miss Joan whose attention he was after. The moment the red-haired owner reached him, Eva and Rachel immediately, albeit reluctantly, stepped aside, giving the older woman unobstructed access to both the babies and the young man who had brought them in.

Deep hazel-green eyes swept over the scene, assessing it. "I assume that there's an explanation why you brought these babies into my diner," Miss Joan said to him.

He nodded. "I was hoping you could tell me who they belonged to."

Miss Joan's austere expression never changed, and neither did her piercing gaze. "You're the one who brought them here, not the other way around. Something you need to get off your chest, boy?" Miss Joan asked him pointedly.

He thought it best if he gave Miss Joan a quick summation of events. Beating around the bush never got anyone anywhere with Miss Joan.

"I found them on the doorstep this morning. Almost walked right on top of them," he told her, giving her all the facts he had to offer. "I've never seen them before and I thought if anyone would know who they belonged to, it would be you."

There was only the barest hint of a smile on the woman's thin lips. "I think you're giving me a little too much credit here, Cole." She looked from one tiny face to the other. "Have they eaten yet?"

"Rosa fed them. I've got a couple of baby bottles all ready to go in the truck," he told her with a hopeful note. Garrett had returned with the bottles from the general store in record time. "So if you or one of your girls want to feed them later—"

"Back up, boy," Miss Joan ordered. "I run a diner, not a nursery." She paused, scrutinizing the expression on his face and putting her own meaning to it. "If you need help later, we can talk. But right now, you've got to find out where these babies came from."

Jeb Campbell, sitting at the counter, raised his hand. "I know where babies come from," he volunteered in all seriousness.

"Eat your eggs, Jeb," she ordered in a no-nonsense voice. "We know where they come from. What we need to know is where they belong. Anyone know of someone who recently gave birth to twins?" she asked, her gaze sweeping over all the occupants of the diner.

It was at that exact moment that the door opened and Stacy walked in.

Silence descended over the entire diner as all eyes turned in Stacy's direction.

As for Stacy, she felt as if she had just walked into one of her nightmares. It was surreal.

Her heart accelerated the second she saw Cole.

And then it all but stopped dead when she saw the babies in the basket. The basket was on the counter, but from its proximity, she assumed that the tiny inhabitants had to belong to Cole.

She'd only been gone from Forever a little over eight months. He certainly didn't waste any time, did he?

Or had he been seeing someone else the entire time he had been seeing her?

Disappointment washed over her like a giant tidal wave. She needed to get out of there, needed to get some air because she could hardly breathe.

Turning on her heel, Stacy was about to push open the door she'd just entered when Miss Joan called out to her.

"Welcome back, Stacy. I was sorry to hear about your aunt."

Stacy froze.

It wasn't her nature not to be polite, no matter how much she wanted to flee. And Miss Joan had just said something nice about Aunt Kate. Stacy couldn't just ignore the woman.

She forced herself to turn around and look at Miss Joan.

How did the woman know? she wondered. No one

knew about her aunt except for Olivia, and she was certain that Olivia wouldn't have said anything. Olivia was a lawyer and prided herself on being discreet.

"Thank you," Stacy finally murmured.

"Park yourself on a stool," Miss Joan instructed. There was no room for argument. "I think Cole here might need some help getting these two little ones over to the clinic."

Cole felt all but numb, seeing Stacy walking into the diner. He'd envisioned this scene a dozen different ways in the last eight months.

More.

Envisioned seeing Stacy walking toward him, tears in her eyes, saying she'd made a mistake leaving. And each and every time, he forgave her. Forgave her because he didn't want to dwell on what had been but rather what could be.

Forgave her because he wanted her in his life.

And now, here she was, back. Back the same day that he had found babies on his doorstep. He looked down at the infants, then up at Stacy.

This couldn't be a coincidence—could it?

Could the babies be hers? And if they were, did that mean…?

Oh, lord, he thought, that would explain so much. Explained why she'd left without a word. Guilt had made her come back, he realized. Guilt because these babies were not only hers, but his, as well.

The thought created elation and panic, and they both vied for equal space within him.

Slowly, the last thing that Miss Joan had just said penetrated the fog around his brain. She was recruiting Stacy to help him take the babies to the clinic.

"The clinic?" he repeated, looking at the woman. "You think they need to be seen by a doctor?"

"You said you found them on your doorstep, right?" Miss Joan reminded him. "It wouldn't hurt to have them checked out—just in case." Miss Joan turned toward Stacy. "Don't you think so?"

"Um, sure." Stacy felt as if she was trying to talk with a tongue that had suddenly grown two sizes. "I don't have any experience with babies and all," Stacy said, pausing uncomfortably between each word. "But that makes sense. I guess."

"Glad that you agree," Miss Joan said in a tone that indicated there was no other path open to either of them except to agree with her. "Why don't you go with Cole and help him?" Again, there was no room for argument. "He certainly can't manage those babies by himself." Before either of them could protest or even comment, Miss Joan asked Cole, "How did you get them over here?"

That he could answer, he thought, relieved. "In my truck."

Miss Joan gave him a withering look. "I realize that. How did you get them over in the truck?"

Cole thought for a second. Miss Joan's interrogation had been known to make many a person's mind go blank. "I secured the basket with ropes and looped them around the passenger seat."

Miss Joan's eyes shifted toward Stacy, the expression on her face indicating that her point had just been made. "Keep an eye on those babies for me," she instructed Stacy.

"I can help," Eva volunteered, stepping forward.

Miss Joan obviously had other ideas about the transport. "Too many cooks spoil the broth," she told the young waitress before looking at Cole and Stacy. "I'm sure these two can manage, working as a team—the way they used to," she added significantly.

Stacy took back her earlier assessment. Hotel or no hotel, nothing had changed in Forever.

The hotel, she suddenly remembered. "I can't go to the clinic."

Miss Joan's expression darkened. "And just why's that?"

"Rebecca just hired me a few minutes ago to work the reception desk," she said quickly, then blurted, "Elsie just found out she's been accepted to college."

Miss Joan looked unconvinced. "College is not for another eleven months," she pointed out.

Stacy shook her head. She could feel Miss Joan beginning to run right over her. "No, she's going in January."

Miss Joan's expression remained unchanged. "Still got time."

Determined, Stacy pushed on. "I know, but she was all excited and took off, quitting right then and there. I told Rebecca I'd take the job."

Cole looked at her in surprise. "You need a job?"

Stacy really didn't feel comfortable discussing anything personal in front of Cole. Not after the way things had gone between them. But with everyone—especially Miss Joan—looking on, she had no choice. She couldn't exactly ignore him.

"It kind of came up," she finally said. "My house burned down, so I'm staying at the hotel."

It was on the tip of his tongue to ask, "Why didn't you come to me?" but in a way he had a feeling that she had, looking at the infants. "If you need a place to stay…" he began.

"Thank you," she said stiffly, cutting him off. "But I just said I have a place to stay. The hotel," she stressed. And then she remembered that she'd only popped over for a quick bite. She needed to be getting back. "Speaking of which—"

There were those who insisted that Miss Joan was part mind reader. Stacy had a tendency to agree.

"Don't worry about it," Miss Joan said, cutting in. "I'll send Rachel over to the hotel to explain what happened. This is September," she reminded the young woman. "Not exactly the busy season for the hotel, so Rebecca should be okay with you not being there for an hour. Or so," she added significantly.

Stacy felt as if things were snowballing out of her control.

"But—" she began to protest.

As if on cue, the babies began to fuss in earnest, each growing progressively louder than the other, as if it was some sort of a pint-sized competition.

Miss Joan nodded toward the infants. "I guess you have your marching orders," she told Cole and Stacy. "Now go. And I don't want to hear anything about you using a rope," she told Cole. "Do I make myself clear?"

"Yes, Miss Joan," he replied.

It was easier that way than getting into an argument with the diner owner. Legend had it that no one had ever won an argument with Miss Joan, and that included her husband, Cash's grandfather. But then, Henry Taylor had doted on Miss Joan, which, it turned out, was exactly the right way to get along with the woman.

"YOU REALLY FOUND these babies on your doorstep?" Stacy asked several minutes later.

She had gotten into the back seat of his truck and he had handed her the wicker basket with the babies. The infants were dozing and the silence in the truck felt overwhelming. Stacy couldn't think of anything else to say, and every other topic would set them off on a course she had no desire to travel.

"Yes, I did," he answered, getting into the driver's seat. He glanced at her over his shoulder.

As if she didn't know where he found the babies, he thought.

He was staring at her, Stacy realized, and it took everything she had not to squirm in her seat. This was a totally bad idea, going with Cole to the clinic like this. But no one said no to Miss Joan and Stacy wasn't about to be the first. She had no desire to have her head handed to her.

"Do you have any idea who the mother might be?" Stacy asked him.

Okay, Cole thought, he'd play along. "There might be a few possibilities," he responded vaguely. "But that's why I came with them to Miss Joan. She's always on top of everything and I figure that she'd be the first to know whose babies they were."

"Miss Joan doesn't know everything," Stacy insisted.

"Maybe," he agreed. "But right now, I figured she was my best shot."

Why are we playing these games, Stacy? Tell me the truth. Are these babies mine?

For one moment, he wrestled with an overwhelming desire to ask the woman in the back seat just that. It would explain why she'd left town so abruptly. But he knew asking her was pointless. He knew her. She wouldn't answer him. In all likelihood, she'd just walk out on him the way she had the last time.

And, angry as he was about her leaving him, he didn't want that happening again. Not until he'd had a chance to talk with her—*really* talk.

Desperate for something to say, he fell back on what Miss Joan had said when she'd first greeted Stacy.

"I'm sorry to hear about your Aunt Kate," he told her. "What happened?"

"She died," Stacy said stoically.

Why are you acting as if you care? We both know you don't. You don't care anything about me or about Aunt Kate, so stop pretending.

"I realize that," he said, doing his best to be patient.

"That's why I said I was sorry to hear about her." Getting his temper under control, he asked, "Did it happen while you were in Europe?"

She looked out the window on her left. "Yes."

He felt pity stirring within him. "That must have been awful for you, having her die and having no one to turn to."

She blew out a breath. She didn't want his sympathy. She didn't want anything from him. Still looking out the side window, she said, "I managed."

"We're here," he announced, and just like that, the topic was closed.

For now.

Chapter Four

Rounding the truck's hood, Cole came to the rear passenger door and opened it before Stacy could. Bending down, he got a firm grip on the wicker basket and drew it out of the truck. The babies were just beginning to wake up again.

"I'll get the door," Stacy volunteered, sliding down off her seat as soon as he had the basket. Before she hurried to the clinic's front door, she paused to look at the babies. One of them was beginning to squirm just enough to throw the basket's weight off while Cole was carrying it. "You want help with that—um, with them?" she corrected.

Was it his imagination, or was she trying too hard to appear unaffected by the sight of the twins? For now, Cole dismissed the thought, but it continued to hover in the back of his mind.

"Just get the door," he told Stacy. "I've got the basket."

For the briefest of moments, Stacy allowed herself a fleeting smile.

"Yes, you do," she said, adding, "You surprise me."

When he raised an eyebrow in silent query, she explained, "I didn't think you'd be any good with babies."

He supposed he could see her point. She hadn't been there to see him with either Devon's baby or the one Cassidy rescued. "I guess we never know what we're capable of until we're confronted with the situation."

"I guess not," she agreed.

It hurt, Cole thought, talking to Stacy like this. The only thing that would hurt more would be *not* being able to talk to her. When she'd suddenly taken off the way she had, he'd thought he would never see her again. He hadn't understood just what hell he'd been in these last eight months until just a few minutes ago, when he saw her walking into Miss Joan's.

Lord, but he'd missed her.

Cole cleared his throat. "Just get the door," he told her gruffly.

Stacy squared her shoulders as she pulled open the front door, then stepped to the side as far as she could, clearing the space for him. The basket was obviously unwieldy, despite his efforts to hold it steady, and she didn't want Cole dropping the babies.

The second they walked in, they became the center of attention.

As usual, the clinic was full. It was the only available medical facility within a fifty-mile radius, so everyone who had a complaint of some sort, or found themselves in need of a checkup, came here. These days there were two doctors on the premises, as well as two nurses. Even so, the clinic was open from around eight, sometimes earlier, until eight, sometimes later. The doors were never officially locked until every patient in the waiting room had been seen.

Initially, the din in the clinic today was a little louder than usual, with fragments of conversations crisscrossing through the air. All that came to an abrupt, startled halt when Cole walked into the reception area carrying the wicker basket with the two babies in it. The fact that Stacy, his former girlfriend, came in right behind him was missed by no one.

Jackson's wife, Debi White Eagle, was behind the desk when they walked in. She immediately rose to her feet, ready to help Cole with the infants he had in the basket.

"Cole, what have you got there?" Debi asked, even though she was actually looking at Stacy when she asked the question.

Cole appeared almost sheepish as he explained, "They were on the doorstep when I left the bunkhouse this morning. I really could have used you," he added, looking at Debi.

Debi had crossed the reception area and was beside him now, getting a closer look at the babies.

"Well, you seem to be doing all right with them," she told Cole with approval. "Whose babies are they?" she asked.

"I don't know," Cole admitted.

His response had a room full of patients murmuring to one another.

"There was no note?" Debi asked, looking from Cole to Stacy.

Cole shook his head. "Nothing," he answered.

Stacy merely shrugged. "I wasn't there."

"If you ask me, I'd say it's finders keepers." Ted Reynolds, an old ranch hand, chuckled.

"The poor darlings," Amanda Rice, the grandmother of three, cooed as she came over to join the widening circle of people admiring the babies. "Where's your mama, darlings?" She raised her eyes to look at Stacy. "And *when* did you come back into town, Stacy?" she asked warmly. "You've been missed," the older woman told her.

"Did you bring the babies in for one of the doctors to examine?" Debi asked, wanting to take control of the situation before things got out of hand.

"Well, yes," Cole confessed, "but I didn't think that there'd be this many people here already." He looked at Debi apologetically. "I've got to get back to my family's ranch—"

"Well, if it helps, you can go ahead of me," Ted Reynolds volunteered. "I've got no real plans for today. Nothing that can't wait, anyway."

"And me," Amanda said. "You can go ahead of me," she told Cole. "At my age, the best part of coming in to see the doctor is socializing with whoever's waiting on him, too."

Several other voices chimed in.

"I can wait," another patient spoke up.

"So can I."

"Me, too. This is the first break from work I've had in over a month," Jeremy Jones said to no one in particular.

Debi held up her hand before anyone else gave up their place to the babies. There were a lot of people in the waiting area and if they all spoke up one by one, this could take a while.

She looked around at the seated people. "Can I assume that it's all right with all of you if I just let Cole go on ahead and bring the babies in to see the doctor?"

A cacophony of voices rose in response to her question. The gist was that the patients in the reception area were all in agreement about letting Cole go in first.

Debi turned toward him. "All right, Cole, you heard them. The people have spoken," she told him cheerfully. "I guess that's why I love living in this town. Everyone's so bighearted.

"Let's get these little darlings checked out. Boys or girls?" she asked, leading the way into the back where the exam rooms were located.

"One of each," Cole answered. As he started to follow the nurse, he looked back over his shoulder toward Stacy. "You coming?"

She was about to beg off, saying something to the effect that it seemed as if he and Debi had the situation covered. But that wasn't strictly true. She knew that Debi had to return to the front desk and even though the other nurse, Holly, was somewhere in the clinic, that still left Cole on his own to cope with two babies. One was probably hard enough for him.

Stacy sighed. She supposed that staying a little longer wouldn't hurt, especially since Miss Joan had said she'd get word to Rebecca at the hotel, explaining about her delay. Given her present situation, the last thing she wanted was to lose her job before she actually started it.

"Yes," she answered, raising her voice, "I'm coming."

Debi opened the door to exam room three. Like the other exam rooms that had been renovated in the clinic, this room was bright and cheery, designed to put the patient in it at ease. Although, Stacy thought, in this case, it really didn't matter.

Debi took out a clipboard with two blank forms attached to it. "Since this is obviously their first visit, I'd normally ask a few routine questions about the patients so we could put the information into their charts." She looked down at the infants and then back at Cole and Stacy. "But I don't suppose you'll be able to answer any of those questions, will you?"

"What kind of questions?" Cole asked, trying to be as helpful as possible.

"The usual ones. Name, date of birth, parents' names, things like that," Debi enumerated.

Feeling a little helpless, Cole had to shake his head. "Can't help you there. You know as much about them as I do."

"That they're cute?" It was a rhetorical question on the nurse's part, asked with a wide smile. "Well," Debi decided after pausing a moment to think, "at least we can put down their weights. Get this little one undressed so I can put him—her—," she corrected once the blanket was unwrapped and Cole began to remove the diaper, "on the scale."

"Aren't they going to get cold?" Cole protested.

"They're not going to be on the scale for that long," Debi assured him.

Stacy was still trying to understand how all this was going to come about.

"How are you going to—oh." The question Stacy had about weighing an infant was answered when she saw Debi place the baby on what looked like an old-fashioned butcher's scale.

Debi smiled, obviously guessing what was going through Stacy's mind. "Might not be state-of-the-art equipment, but it gets the job done for these little ones." After jotting down the number from the scale, she lifted the naked infant and handed her to Stacy. "Definitely not undernourished," she pronounced. "That's a good sign. Why don't you put her diaper and blanket back on and I'll weigh the other one," she told Stacy, then turned her attention to the second infant. "You said this one's a boy, right?" she asked Cole.

"Right," he responded, glad to be able to contribute at least something to the process. "Rosa fed and diapered both of them before I came here. That woman's fantastic."

"That's exactly how we feel about her," Debi agreed. "Don't know where we'd be without her." Once she'd removed the second infant's blanket and diaper, she placed him on the scale. He whimpered in protest. "Guess he doesn't care for the feel of metal against his skin." She jotted down the weight she read on the scale, then glanced at Stacy. "How're we doing over there?" she asked.

It was obvious that Stacy was having more than a little difficulty in putting the diaper back on the infant.

"I don't know about *we*," Stacy said, exasperated, "but *I'm* not doing too well."

The infant seemed to be all moving arms and legs and Stacy was having trouble getting the diaper to stay on her.

Putting down the second chart she was filling in, Debi made quick work of rediapering the first infant. Stacy looked on, chagrined.

"It just takes practice," the nurse said matter-of-factly.

"How's this?" Cole asked, holding up the baby he'd attempted to diaper.

As if on cue, the diaper began a rather quick descent down the second infant's chubby little hips.

"You've almost got it, Cole," Debi told him, taking the baby from Cole and quickly refastening the diaper tabs.

After diapering the newest patients, Debi loosely swaddled each infant and placed one in Cole's arms and one in Stacy's, much to their surprise.

"There's no sense in wrapping them up in their blankets just yet," she told the duo. "The doctor will only have to unwrap them to do his exam." Debi was about to leave when she paused and turned around. "Have either of you come up with any names we could put on the charts for the time being?" She glanced over toward the charts. "Baby Boy Doe and Baby Girl Doe just sound so terribly lonely."

Cole had his doubts about doing that. "Do you think it's right, naming them?" he asked. "I mean, we're bound to find the parents."

A rather bemused smile curved Debi's mouth. She was originally from Chicago and had worked in a city hospital where a much harsher reality prevailed. Parents didn't always come back for their children. She'd had experience with babies being abandoned, left on the hospital doorstep without a backward glance and never reclaimed.

But she had come to know a kinder, gentler reality in Forever, and she really hoped that it would win out in this instance, as it had in others.

"I know," Debi said, smiling at the two people in the exam room. "This would only be temporary. I just think that it would just make things—more personal. Any ideas as to names?" she asked, looking from Cole to Stacy.

Cole debated saying anything. And then, before he knew it, he heard himself suggesting, "How about Kate for the girl?" He looked at Stacy when he offered the name.

"Kate," Stacy repeated. She could feel a warmth growing within her, as well as gratitude toward Cole for having suggested it. Very quietly, she said, "Aunt Kate would have liked that." Then, speaking up, Stacy said, "Yes, sure, why not?"

"All right, then. Kate it is," Debi pronounced. Picking up the appropriate chart, she wrote the name on top of the paper. Picking up the second chart, she asked, "And the boy?"

Stacy looked at Cole. She appreciated the fact that he had just paid her late aunt a compliment by naming the infant girl after her. Turnabout was only fair play.

"How about Mike?" she asked, looking at Debi.

Mike, Stacy knew, had been Cole's father's name. From the stories that she'd heard Cole tell, he and his siblings had all been close to the hardworking man who had raised them.

Cole pressed his lips together, getting control over his emotions. "Sounds good," Cole agreed, nodding his head.

"Okay, so now we have names for them. Temporarily," Debi added, more for Cole and Stacy's benefit than for accuracy. "I'll tell Dr. Davenport you're here," she told them. "I think he's the next one free—unless you want Dr. Cordell to see them."

"No, Dr. Davenport's fine," Cole assured her.

Daniel Davenport, a New York transplant, had been the one to reopen the clinic. Prior to that, the clinic had been closed for more than thirty years. The doctor had been the first to tell people that he didn't come halfway across the country to reopen the clinic out of any selfless devotion to his profession. He'd initially wanted to be a surgeon attached to one of the more well-known, prestigious hospitals in New York. It was his younger brother who had been the dedicated one, and he was the doctor who was supposed to come to Forever.

But the night before his brother was to leave, Dan had convinced him to go out for one last celebratory drink. On the way home, a drunk driver had plowed into their car. Dan had gotten away with a few scratches. His brother hadn't been so lucky. He'd died at the scene.

Guilt had made Dan come out to the tiny Texas town in the middle of nowhere in his brother's place, but only until he could find a suitable replacement.

That had been a number of years ago, and since then, Dan had made a life for himself here in Forever—and now he said that it was the best decision he had ever made.

A tall, robust man who seemed to thrive on the long hours he put in, Dr. Davenport came into the room less than two minutes after Debi had left.

"I hear Forever has two brand-new citizens," he said, crossing to the exam table where Stacy and Cole were watching over the two infants. The babies were lying side by side, taking in the world around them in wide-eyed wonder.

Dan nodded at Stacy. "Nice to see you back in Forever, Stacy. You're looking a little paler than I remember. Are you feeling all right?"

"I'm fine, Doctor," she said almost defensively. "I'm just here to help with the babies."

"Well, then, I'd better get to it and make sure these

babies are as healthy as they look," Dan said, turning his attention to the infant closer to him.

Stacy breathed a subtle sigh of relief, glad the focus was off her.

Chapter Five

"I'm happy to tell you that both of these little people appear to be in good health," Dan told Cole and Stacy as he put away his stethoscope and the other instruments he had used to check out the babies' state of well-being.

"Doc, about how old would you say they were?" Cole asked.

Dan laughed softly as he considered the question. "Well, unfortunately, babies aren't like trees. You can't just check their rings. There is no surefire way to ascertain just how old they are, but going by experience, I'd say that these two appear to be approximately three weeks old."

"And you don't recognize them?" Cole pressed hopefully.

Dan regarded the man next to him. "Do you mean have I seen them before because their mother or father brought them in?" He saw the hopeful expression that came into Cole's eyes, but he had to shake his head. "Sorry, these two have never been here before. I definitely would have remembered twins," he added.

Cole wasn't ready to give up just yet. "What if they were brought in one at a time?"

Dan smiled kindly at the cowboy. "Now you're really reaching, Cole—but I'm afraid my answer's still the same." He glanced at the twins, back on the exam table with Cole and Stacy positioned on either side of them again. "I've never seen them before."

Kate was wiggling and she managed to loosen the blanket that had been tucked around her after her exam was completed. Dan observed with approval as Stacy refastened the blanket around the infant.

"Have you tried bringing them to Miss Joan?" he suggested.

"Yes," Cole replied, a touch of dejection in his voice. "No luck."

Dan thought of his brother-in-law, Rick Santiago. "You could try the sheriff, I guess. If Rick doesn't recognize them, either, he might still be able to locate the mother—or the father. I would imagine that either would do in this case."

"Would they?" Stacy asked, speaking up. "I mean, if these babies were abandoned, then maybe neither one of the parents is the right person to leave them with—even if we could find them."

"You might have a point, but I think that at least to begin with, they should be given the benefit of the doubt," Dan told them.

There was a knock on the exam room door. No one came in, but Dan obviously knew who was on the other side.

"Listen, if you still have any questions for me and want to talk, why don't you drop by after hours when the clinic is closed? But right now, I've got a waiting room full of patients to see, so I'm going to have to cut this discussion short. Keep me posted," he told them, his glance sweeping over both people. "And let me know if you find their mother—or father."

Dan closed the door behind him.

The moment he did, Cole looked at the infants, who were now back in the wicker basket, nestled against each other.

"Now what?" Stacy asked.

"Well, pretty soon I'd say we're going to need a bigger basket for these two. But for now, I guess we'll do what Dr. Dan suggested and go talk to Sheriff Santiago."

"You think *he's* going to recognize them?" she asked dubiously.

Cole frowned slightly. "I take it by the skepticism in your voice, you don't think he will."

"Highly doubtful," Stacy responded. "Unless someone reported them kidnapped—at which point I think Dr. Dan probably would have known about them."

He supposed that she had a point. But Forever was growing and communication wasn't what it used to be, so there was a chance that the sheriff might be able to help.

"Still, I think the sheriff should know that they were abandoned," he told Stacy, smiling down at Mike. As he spoke, he gently slid his finger against Mike's cheek.

Reaching up, the infant wrapped his tiny fingers around it. And around Cole's heart, as well.

Stacy took that a step further. "So he can arrest the mother if he finds her? Is that really the way you want to go with this?"

Cole had been all set to pick up the basket and walk out of the exam room with the babies, but Stacy's comment stopped him. He hadn't even considered that possibility occurring.

"When did you get so pessimistic about things?" he demanded.

Stacy made no answer, she merely fixed a laser-like glare on him. He decided it was best not to pursue the matter, at least for now.

Instead, after first opening the door, he picked up the basket and made his way back to the reception area. Stacy was right behind him.

Any thoughts of a fast getaway were quickly aborted. The moment they walked out to the front of the clinic, they were engulfed in questions.

"Did Dr. Dan recognize them?"

"If he didn't, maybe Dr. Alisha knows who they are."

"Did the babies check out okay?"

"What are you going to do with them now?"

Because Cole looked as if he was a little overwhelmed with the barrage of questions, Stacy decided to run interference for both of them.

"No, Dr. Dan didn't recognize the twins," she told one woman. "Dr. Alisha didn't come in to consult, but I'm sure he would have called her in if he thought she might have recognized them. And both of the babies are the picture of health," she told the people in the waiting room with an air of finality. She'd really thought that would be sufficient enough to get them out of the clinic, or at least to the door.

But then Lyle Henderson, a big, burly rancher, spoke up, repeating the last question. "So what are you going to do with them now?"

"We're taking them to the sheriff," Cole answered.

"A little young to be behind bars, aren't they?" Duke Crenshaw asked with a booming laugh that temporarily blocked out everything else.

It also managed to wake up the babies.

Duke's wife, who had driven her husband over to the clinic, hit his shoulder with the back of her hand. Given that she was somewhat bigger than her husband, the blow stung and Duke yelped.

"Serves you right. See what you've done? You woke them up," Mrs. Crenshaw berated him.

"No harm done," Cole tossed over his shoulder as he quickly left the clinic with the twins before any further questions threatened to keep them there longer.

"I guess nothing *has* changed," Stacy said as they walked over to his truck.

Her comment seemed to have come out of nowhere. "How so?"

She nodded toward the clinic. "It seems like everybody in Forever is still minding everybody else's business."

"They're just concerned," Cole told her.

"They're just nosy."

"Speaking of being nosy…" Cole began, setting the basket down next to him on the ground in order to open the rear passenger door. "How are you doing?"

Stacy climbed into the back seat and waited for him to hand her the basket, or at least secure it on the floor beside her feet, the way he had earlier.

"What do you mean?" she asked guardedly. She had the uneasy feeling he was trying to make a point, but he kept skirting the issue.

"I mean how are you doing?" Cole repeated.

It didn't sound like such a hard question to answer, he thought. When Stacy continued to look at him blankly, Cole elaborated. He tried to do it carefully because he didn't want to accidentally make things worse by saying the wrong thing or by phrasing things so that they opened fresh wounds.

In the end, Cole wound up being blunt because, no matter how much he aspired to it, finesse wasn't exactly his forte.

"Your aunt died while the two of you were traveling together. That had to have been a great shock for you to deal with."

Stacy squared her shoulders, frowning. "We already covered this."

"No, we didn't," he contradicted. "Not in the way you mean. I told you I was sorry to hear about your aunt and asked what happened. You said she died and that you managed. That's not talking about it," Cole said, closing her door for her.

Rounding the back of the truck, Cole came around to his side of the vehicle. He got into the driver's seat and closed his door.

"Yes it is," Stacy insisted, struggling not to raise her voice and agitate the twins. "It's just not talking it to death."

He wasn't ready to put the subject to rest. "You were traveling in a foreign country. You must have felt awful when it happened."

"Well, I wasn't about to dance a jig. Aunt Kate was my only remaining family and she'd always been there for me. She was the one I always turned to for guidance. And suddenly she wasn't there to guide me anymore." Stacy stopped, realizing that she had said too much and that she was on the verge of tears.

She wasn't about to cry in front of anyone, least of all Cole.

This was what she got for coming back, she thought, upbraiding herself.

"That's what I mean. It must have been really awful for you," he said sympathetically, wishing he could have been there for her. "I just want you to know that I'm here if you want to talk about it."

Stacy frowned, looking down at the babies rather than at him. "I just did."

"That wasn't really talking, Stacy."

She blew out a breath, annoyed. "There were no hand puppets involved. Lips were moving. Words were said. As far as I'm concerned, that's considered talking," she informed him with finality. "Let's concentrate on finding these babies' parents and not on anything that happened in the past, all right? There's the sheriff's office." Stacy pointed out the window toward the building on the right.

"I know," he answered. "I'm familiar with it. That's where I was headed."

"Well, congratulations," she told him with a touch of sarcasm. "You've reached it."

Okay, he'd been patient enough, he thought. "Why are you mad at me?" he asked. "I'm the one who should be mad at you."

Stunned, she felt her mouth drop open before she could get control over herself.

"In what universe?" Stacy demanded.

"In this one," he retorted.

Her temper flashed and it took everything she had to rein it in.

"You know what," she said between clenched teeth, "let's just table this and bring the babies in to the sheriff before I forget I'm a lady and really say something ugly."

With that, she didn't wait for Cole to come around to open her door. She opened the opposite passenger door and got out, then quickly hurried to the other side to get the babies out before Cole could reach them.

He arrived at the same time she did. Seeing what she was up to, he glared at her. "Now you're being pigheaded," he told her.

"You always did have a silver tongue," she said sweetly.

Cole shook his head. "And to think I actually thought I missed you."

"Yeah," she retorted, "I was just thinking the same thing."

He blew out a breath, telling himself that it wouldn't do either one of them—or more importantly, the twins—any good to blow up like this right here in front of the sheriff's office. It was just that he had forgotten just how easily Stacy could set him off, and half the time—like now—she did it without warning. It was like being caught in a blitzkrieg.

She was obviously angry at him and he had no clue as to why or what was going on in her head. But then, that was nothing new, either.

"Stacy," he said, growing stern, "let me take the basket in. It's heavy."

Stacy stubbornly stood her ground and kept her fingers around the edges of the basket, refusing to release it. "I can manage."

He'd gotten some insight over the years about how to approach at least a few subjects when it came to Stacy. "Nobody's disputing that, but I think it would be better for the babies if I carried the basket."

"It's not heavy," she argued. Except that it really was. And the babies were moving. With a sigh, she relented. "It's awkward."

"All the more reason for me to take it in," Cole told her. The woman, he thought, was as stubborn as she was beautiful. That hadn't changed.

For a few brief seconds, she debated continuing to

argue the point with him. There was just something about Cole; he pressed all her buttons. He always had. No matter what she tried to tell herself, that much hadn't changed.

But her arms *were* beginning to really ache. So, in the end, she said, "Fine, you can carry them in—but only because I'm thinking of the babies."

Tempted to smile, he refrained. Instead, he said, "I understand."

"Don't patronize me, Cole."

There went his temper again, snapping like an old-fashioned slingshot. "Damn it, woman, you can get my blood boiling the way nobody else ever could."

Ignoring the gist of what Cole had just said, she focused on the words he'd used. "Don't swear in front of the babies."

"They won't *remember*," he stressed. All he wanted to do was go inside the sheriff's office and make these twins someone else's problem.

"I don't want to put that theory to the test," she countered.

"Why not?" Cole demanded. "You don't seem to have any qualms about testing me."

Her eyes narrowed. "Because you're not a sweet infant."

He opened his mouth, ready to tell her off. But then he stopped.

They were here, at the sheriff's door, and any further discussion, sharp-tongued or otherwise, was going to have to be put on hold unless they wanted to have the sheriff suddenly coming out of the office and acting as a referee.

As if on cue, they both stopped bickering.

Stacy opened the door of the sheriff's office. "After you," she said sweetly, stepping to one side so that Cole could enter first, carrying the babies in the basket.

Spying only the basket that Cole was carrying, Rick Santiago called out, "I hope you brought me something from Miss Joan's Diner," from across the room as he headed toward the duo.

"I don't think this qualifies as lunch, Sheriff," Joe Lone Wolf commented. His was the first desk that Cole and Stacy passed when they entered the office and he'd gotten a good look at the contents of the basket.

"Hey, welcome back, Stacy," Cody McCullough, Cole's younger brother declared, greeting her. "It's nice seeing you again."

One look at the babies and Cody appeared to reassess the situation. Stunned, Cody's eyes darted toward Stacy, then back to his brother. "You two come here to make some kind of an announcement?"

"Yeah," Cole said, guessing at what was going through Cody's head. "That I've got an idiot for a younger brother."

"Then these babies aren't…?" Cody looked from Cole to Stacy again and then back to the babies.

"No!" Cole said firmly, placing the basket on Joe's desk.

Cole knew he was vehemently denying parentage, but the simple truth was that he wasn't all that sure that these babies weren't his. If nothing else, the timing seemed to be right. Stacy had been gone for eight months. But she wasn't acting like she was their mother.

"Sheriff," Cole said to the tall, dark-haired man who had crossed the office to approach them. "These babies were left on my doorstep this morning and we were hoping you could help us find their mother."

He spared one quick look in Stacy's direction to see if what he was about to say was going to affect her in any manner. Her face appeared impassive.

"Otherwise, I'm going to have to bring them to social services over in Mission Ridge."

"You're going to do what?" Stacy cried, stunned. She pulled the basket protectively closer to her.

Chapter Six

Stacy noticed that her voice had gone up and she took a second to collect herself. She couldn't believe that Cole would be so dismissive of these babies, even though they did eventually need a real home.

"But you're going to wait to give the sheriff time to investigate, right?" she asked Cole, giving him a chance to redeem himself.

"Sure," he answered. "That's why we came here to see him."

Stacy had a strange expression on her face he couldn't quite fathom. He found himself going back to wondering if the babies were hers.

"One question." Rick held up his hand to get their attention.

Still wondering about Stacy's reaction, Cole glanced toward the sheriff. "Go ahead, Sheriff."

Rick indicated the babies in the basket. "What are you going to do with these two little ones while you're waiting to find out if the deputies and I can locate their mama somewhere?"

Cole wasn't following what the sheriff was asking. "What do you mean?"

"Where are they going to be staying?"

Instead of answering Rick's question, Cole turned to look at his brother. After Cody had helped a stranded Devon give birth to her baby, he'd wound up taking her in and she'd lived at the family ranch until Cody and she had gotten married.

"Um—Cody?"

Cody immediately seemed to pick up on the hopeful note in his brother's voice. "Oh, no, sorry. I'm going to have to pass. Devon's already got her hands full."

Cole turned toward Stacy next. Given how passionate she'd sounded about not taking the twins to social services, maybe she was willing to take them in for the time being.

"Stacy?"

Stacy raised her hands up, as if to physically block any arguments Cole could come up with.

"I can help out—when I'm not working," she told him. "I can't take them in. I don't even have a permanent place to stay myself. I'm staying at the hotel."

"Well, it's not like I'm not working," Cole protested. She hadn't even started her job. He had been at his for years. "Technically, I've actually got two jobs. I work part-time at the Healing Ranch and the rest of the time with Connor on our ranch, so I'm pretty much busy all the time."

"Then I'd say that these two little people have a problem," Rick concluded, cutting into the discussion. He slanted a glance at Cole and then at Stacy.

"You could take them with you to the ranch," Stacy argued, looking right at Cole. "Connor's still there, right?"

Cole frowned. He didn't like the way this was being twisted. "Well, he's kind of in charge, so yes, he's still there." He knew what was coming next. "But he's busy working the ranch, just like I am," Cole emphasized.

Joe sat up in his chair a little straighter. "You've still got that housekeeper, don't you?" Joe asked, then added her name in for good measure. "Rita."

Cody laughed. "Just when I think you're not listening to a word I say," he marveled, looking at the other deputy. "Son of a gun, you really *are* paying attention."

Joe wore the same emotionless expression he always did. "I don't have to look like I'm hanging on your every word in order to be listening, McCullough," Joe said quietly.

It was time to wrap this up before it dragged on for hours. "All right," Rick declared, directing his words toward Cole. "Then it's settled. These two," he nodded at the twins, "are going to be staying at your ranch and Rita's going to be looking after them for a bit, with help from you, your brother and Stacy."

"But—" Cole started to protest.

Rick cut him short. "If I'm going to be doing my job, trying to find these kids' mama, I don't have time to be arguing with you, Cole," the sheriff told him. "Now you take those kids on home to your place and tell Connor I'll be talking to him when I get a chance."

With that, Rick retreated into his office to make a few calls.

Cody saw the expression on his brother's face. "It's not so bad," he assured Cole. "Remember what it was like when I brought Devon and her baby to the ranch to stay with us?"

"What I remember is a lot of crying," Cole reminded his brother.

Cody grinned at him. "Yeah, but you got over it and stopped." Joe and Stacy laughed at his comment.

"Very funny," Cole retorted. He looked down at the twins, resigned. "Well, I guess I'd better bring these two to the ranch and hope that Rita's in one of her good moods."

Cody waved his hand at his brother's concern. "Rita loves babies. Remember how good she was with the one Cassidy saved from the creek when we had that big flash flood?"

Joe snorted and shook his head. "That makes a total of four babies, counting these. You McCulloughs are regular baby magnets, you know that?"

Rather than address the ribbing remark Joe had just made, Cole glanced at the senior deputy. A full-blooded Navajo, Joe Lone Wolf had been raised on the reservation that was located about fifteen miles south of the outskirts of Forever. Although he was married to the town vet, the sheriff's sister, Ramona, and lived in the town proper, Joe went back to the reservation regularly in order to visit.

"Hey, Joe," Cole began hesitantly, "do you think that you could ask around on the reservation, see if maybe these babies belong to one of the girls there?"

Rather than answering immediately, Joe scrutinized the infants that had been placed on his desk.

"I can ask around, see if anyone knows anything," he remarked.

His tone indicated that he doubted the infants belonged to anyone from the reservation.

"Thanks. I'm just covering all the bases for now," Cole told the deputy as he picked up the basket again. One of the twins made a squealing noise. "Okay, you two, time for you to meet Connor."

As he started for the door, he caught a movement out of the corner of his eye. Stacy had gone around him in order to open the door.

"Thanks," he murmured. When she continued walking beside him, he stopped for a second. "Are you coming with me?"

Did he think she was shadowing him for some ulterior motive? "Yes, I'm coming with you," she answered. "I said I'd help out, and since my first day of work was postponed until tomorrow, thanks to Miss Joan, I've got the time to help—unless you've got this covered and don't want me to come over," she added.

"No. I mean yes. I mean—" Frustrated, Cole blew out an annoyed breath. Why did he always get things so muddled up when she was around? "Oh, hell, just get in the truck. I'll drive you home when you're ready to go," he added before they could get tangled up in a discussion about how she was going to get back to town.

Stacy frowned, looking at the twins in the basket. "You're not supposed to be cursing in front of those babies," she reminded him.

"I'm not supposed to be doing a lot of things I'm doing," he told her.

Rather than just let his remark go, she challenged him.

"Just what's that supposed to mean?" Stacy wanted to know.

I'm not supposed to be letting you get to me the way you are, but it's happening anyway, even though I know you'll just wind up stomping on my heart again the way you did the first time.

The remark burned on his tongue, but he bit it back. No sense in rehashing things.

"Nothing," he answered curtly, then practically growled, "I appreciate the help." After taking a breath, he continued more calmly. "As do Mike and Kate." Opening the rear passenger door, he tucked the babies' basket in on the floor again, the way he had before.

On the opposite side, Stacy took a seat and looked down at the small, round faces. Cole made his way to the driver's side and got in.

"What do you think their real names are?" she asked Cole.

Was that just for his benefit, or didn't she really

know? He kept vacillating as to whether or not she was actually their mother.

"I don't know," he replied, starting up his truck. "Maybe their mother didn't bother naming them. Maybe she figured naming them would just humanize them for her and she didn't want to get close to them."

"That's awfully cold," she commented. Especially coming from him, Stacy added silently. Cole usually saw the best in everyone. It was one of the things she'd liked best about him.

"So's leaving two infants on someone's doorstep," Cole countered.

Stacy was silent for a moment, thinking. And then she said, "I don't know, maybe their mother was desperate and she knew that you were a good person who would take care of them. That you'd make sure they were all right."

Damn it, this was going to drive him crazy. *Was it you, Stacy? Did you leave these babies on that doorstep because you knew I'd be there this morning? Are these our babies, yours and mine?*

He really wanted to ask her that.

The questions hovered on the tip of his tongue. But something told him that now wasn't the time to ask. Besides, even if he did ask her and she said no, would he believe her? He didn't know. It was better if he put off asking Stacy so he could watch her interact with Kate and Mike first.

Maybe she'd give herself away if he was patient enough.

"Why me?" he asked her out of the blue. Raising his eyes to the rearview mirror, he saw her looking at him quizzically. "Connor's the more responsible one, raising the three of us the way he did. Why not leave the babies with him?"

He saw her shrug. "I don't know. Maybe it was proximity."

He didn't follow. "What?"

"Proximity," Stacy repeated. "Maybe the babies' mother lived closer to the Healing Ranch than your family's ranch," she speculated. And then she rethought her response. "But I think the real answer's simpler than that," she told him.

"Oh? So what is the simpler answer?" Cole asked. Maybe the more he got her to talk about the twins, the more likely she'd be to admit that she was the one who'd left them on his doorstep—if she actually had.

"Their mother picked you, not Connor," Stacy stressed for a second time, "because she knew you were a good person."

He felt he had to come to his brother's defense. "Connor's a good person." All things considered, Connor was probably the best person he knew.

"I don't know, maybe she didn't know Connor. What difference does it make why?" she asked, losing patience. "The point is that she picked you to leave her babies with."

If she hadn't been the one to leave them, then there was a different way to look at the whole thing. "Maybe she just abandoned them and left them some place she figured they'd be found."

Stacy sighed. "Maybe. And maybe not. The point is that you have them, Cole."

"For now," he reminded her, thinking back to what he'd said about taking the twins to social services as a last resort.

Stacy drew back her shoulders and became rigid. "You weren't serious about what you said before." Her voice lowered to almost an ominous level. "Were you?"

He was preoccupied with what he was going to say to Connor when he took the babies in. He heard her, but her words didn't really register.

"You're going to have to be more specific than that," he told Stacy.

He knew damn well what she was referring to, she thought. Why was he playing games like this?

"That if the sheriff doesn't find their mother, you're going to bring those babies to the social services office in Mission Ridge," she said, her jaw all but clenched.

"That would be the best place for them," he pointed out matter-of-factly.

"No, it wouldn't," she argued, her voice growing louder. "How can you say something like that after the way Connor gave up his dream of going to college just to become your guardian so that you and your brother and sister didn't wind up being taken in by the system?" she demanded.

"Connor was family," he explained, then pointed out,

"These kids might not have a family. Social services could find a home for them."

"They could also split them up," she retorted with passion. "There aren't that many people who are willing to take on two kids at the same time."

"How would you know?" Cole asked, dismissing her protest.

The words rushed out of her mouth before Stacy realized she was saying them. Words that gave away the secret she'd guarded so zealously for as long as she could remember. Guarded because she didn't want people looking at her differently. Above all, she didn't want people pitying her.

"Because I had a twin sister and my mother left us with social services."

"What are you talking about?" Cole demanded. "I knew your mother. She was one of the kindest women I ever met." He remembered thinking that if his mother had lived, she would have been just like Sally Rowe.

"That was my adoptive mother, not my real mother," Stacy told him.

Stunned, he raised his eyes to the rearview mirror again. "You were adopted?"

"See, you're already thinking differently of me." Even in the mirror, she could see what he was thinking.

"Only because you never told me," he said, trying to wrap his head around the revelation. "How could you not tell me?" They'd been so close, sharing dreams, sharing secrets—and all this time, she'd kept this from him. He felt as if everything he'd once thought they'd had had been built on sand. "And what's this about a twin sister?" he asked. "Where is she now?"

Stacy steeled herself off before she was able to answer his question. She'd brought this on herself. But she couldn't just ignore his question after what she'd just said.

"She died," Stacy answered stoically. "They separated us and placed us with different foster parents. Turns out that the people my sister was staying with believed in severe punishment for any minor disobedience." Her voice began to tremble and she had to take a moment to regain control. "My sister's punishment turned out to be fatally severe."

Cole pulled his truck over to the side of the road so he could turn around and really look at her. Thrown for a loop, he didn't want to risk driving into a ditch. "How old were you?"

Stacy laced her fingers together and stared at them, unable to look at Cole, afraid of what she might see in his eyes.

"I was five. Old enough to remember her. And to understand that I was never going to see her again. The memory was too painful, so I blocked it all out. My mother—the woman I called my mother," she stressed, "knew all this when she and my...my father adopted me." A sad smile curved her mouth as she went on looking down at her hands. "She did everything she could to help me adjust." Stacy's voice became a little steadier as she added, "She also saw to it that that other family was brought up on manslaughter charges. They were found guilty. I didn't know that at the time, but I found out about it later. My mother told me when she thought I was old enough to be able to understand."

He wanted to hold her. To tell her he was sorry. But he knew Stacy would only withdraw into herself. Still, he had to know. "Why didn't you tell me?"

Stacy squared her shoulders and looked up. "I just did."

"But I mean *then*," he stressed. "When we were going together."

The short laugh had no mirth to it. "Not exactly a story that's meant for sharing," she told him.

"But you told me now," he pointed out. If she told him now, she could have told him then.

"I told you now because I don't want you even *thinking* about handing these babies over to social services yet. Granted there are some very nice people out there who want to open their homes up to a child—but that's not always the case. I know that you need to find out more about them first before you take the risk."

Her eyes met his. Hers had an intensity to them he'd never seen before. "Promise me you won't take them to social services right away?"

"I promise," he told her. But he wanted her to understand the full import of what she was asking. "What if the sheriff can't find their parents?"

"I'll think of something," she told him. Exactly what, she wasn't sure, but anything was better than the kind of life that her twin had so briefly had. "Now start driving," Stacy ordered.

Cole saw tear tracks on her cheeks.

But he knew better than to point that out or say anything about them. Instead, he took out his handkerchief and passed it back to her, then started up his truck again.

He thought he heard her murmur, "Thanks," but he wasn't sure. The twins had started fussing and they were drowning Stacy out.

Cole couldn't help thinking that he was heading to the ranch—and Rita—just in time.

Chapter Seven

Cole walked into the ranch house he had thought of as home for his entire life. He couldn't begin to imagine what it had to be like for children who hadn't been as lucky as his siblings and him.

Until today, he had never thought of Stacy as even remotely being in that sort of a category. He'd never had a clue that she'd known anything but security throughout her whole life.

You just never knew.

The living room was empty.

He guessed that Connor was most likely out on the range, tending to whatever problem had come up today. Just as well, he thought. He'd face his brother with the news of this latest development after the twins were taken care of.

"Rita, are you home?" Cole called out, raising his voice.

"I'm in the kitchen, Mr. Cole," Rita answered, her almost melodic, accented voice floating through the rooms. "Do you need something?"

"You could say that," Cole replied. He walked into the kitchen with the babies.

Rita's back was to the doorway. Moving between the stove and the counter, she was in the midst of preparing dinner. Because she never knew just how many people would be seated at the dinner table, the woman Cole and Connor had considered a godsend ever since she joined the household always made sure that she prepared plenty. The whole family agreed that even Rita's leftovers were beyond good. The woman clearly had a gift. Cody had once said the housekeeper could make three-day-old dirt taste delicious.

"Well, what is it?" Rita asked, chopping furiously and reducing celery stalks into tiny bits of green.

"Turn around, please," Cole requested.

Putting down the huge knife she was wielding with the expertise of a master swordsman, the housekeeper deposited the diced celery into the large pot of stew she had on the back burner and then turned away from the stove.

"Speak quickly, please. I have work to do," Rita told Cole before she fully turned around to face him.

Her dark eyes widening, Rita stared at the basket the rancher was holding. Within less than half a second, the older woman was melting.

Wiping her hands on the apron around her middle, she came forward, her eyes never leaving the infants. "What do you have there?"

"Babies," Cole answered. "Twins to be more accurate."

Rita was already beaming at the infants. "Whose?" she asked as she tickled Kate's tummy. Kate made a noise that was very close to a giggle.

"That's just it," Cole said after sparing a glance at Stacy for any last-moment intervention. Stacy said nothing so he told the housekeeper, "We don't know."

"Miss Stacy," Rita greeted the young woman beside Cole politely. She recognized her from a photograph Cole still had in his room. Asking around, the housekeeper had become aware of the backstory. "Are you here for a visit?"

"No, to stay," Stacy told her. Then, to be strictly honest, she added, "For now."

Sharp dark eyes darted from the infants toward the woman she'd just greeted. "Did you bring these babies with you?" Rita asked.

"No, she's just here to help out," Cole explained. The twins' fussing had gone up a notch, increasing in volume. "I think they're hungry. Or maybe they need changing again."

He raised his eyes, looking at the housekeeper. It was clear that he felt out of his depth and was silently asking for her help.

A knowing look came into Rita's eyes. "And you would like me to see which it is?"

He nodded, looking at her sheepishly. "Something like that."

"So, then, they will be staying here?" Rita asked. She paused to turn the burner beneath the large stew pot down to low. The stew needed to simmer for a couple of hours before it was ready.

"For the time being," Cole told her. "They don't have anywhere else to go," he added, hoping that would win the woman over completely.

"I see. Does Mr. Connor know?" she asked.

"I told him about finding the babies, but no, I didn't say anything about having them stay here," Cole admitted.

Rita nodded. "He is a smart man, Mr. Connor. He has probably already guessed as much." Rita picked up the baby closest to her. It turned out to be Mike. Taking a deep whiff, she said, "Oh, yes, this one needs to be changed." She looked at Cole. "Did you by any chance bring any diapers with you?"

"Yes," he answered, happy that he'd at least gotten this right. "Garrett picked up diapers for them at the general store, along with a couple of baby bottles and some formula," he told her, then added, "Rosa sent him out with a list. Everything's in the truck right now. I'll just go out and get it."

"You said something about *finding* them?" Rita asked him, curious.

"They were on my doorstep." Cole tossed the words over his shoulder as he hurried out the front door to his truck.

With Cole gone, Rita turned to look at Stacy. Her expression indicated that she was waiting to be filled in on the rest of the story.

Stalling and uncomfortable, Stacy went to pick up

the second twin. Kate stopped fussing the second she was in Stacy's arms and laid her small head on Stacy's shoulder.

An immense feeling of contentment and satisfaction filled Stacy. It surprised her as much as it pleased her.

"He found these babies on his doorstep?" Rita pressed. "I don't understand. Mr. Cole's doorstep is here. He didn't find them here," she stated.

"I think he meant he found them outside the room he stays in at the Healing Ranch," Stacy explained, although she really didn't know much about that situation. From what she had pieced together, she'd learned that Cole had begun working at the Healing Ranch after she left town.

Rita shook her head, her features softening with sympathy. "Someone left these poor little lambs out in the cold? They could have gotten very sick. Who would do such a heartless thing?" she demanded, cradling Mike against her ample bosom.

"Maybe a mother who was desperate," Stacy ventured. She didn't want to sound as if she was taking sides, but there was obviously more than one side to this situation. Seeing the less than sympathetic expression on the housekeeper's face, she quickly added, "The sheriff is trying to find their mother."

Wanting to avoid Rita's condemning gaze, Stacy gazed down at Kate. As she did so, she caught herself smiling.

"You like babies." It wasn't a question on Rita's part but a judgment.

"I suppose," Stacy said, not wanting to commit herself one way or the other. "They haven't become people yet."

Rita looked as if she was considering what she'd just heard. "Then you have been hurt," Rita concluded.

She knew the other woman by sight, but Rita hadn't yet come to work for the McCulloughs when Cole and Stacy had been involved. Rita studied the young woman's face, making her own assumptions from what she was even now piecing together.

"No more than anyone else," Stacy answered vaguely. Trying to appear aloof, she deliberately put distance between herself and the other woman. She had the feeling that Rita could see right through her and she didn't want anyone in her head.

"I've got diapers, bottles and milk, and Garrett picked up a couple of pacifiers, too," Cole announced, holding two large paper bags aloft.

Walking back into the house quickly, he placed both of the bags on the kitchen table and leaned one against the other so they wouldn't accidentally spill out their contents.

"What about a change of clothes?" Rita asked him.

He looked at her, slightly bewildered. "What about it?"

Rita pressed her full lips together, searching for patience. "Do you have any in those bags that you brought in?"

"I don't think Rosa told him to get any change of clothes for the babies," he told the housekeeper.

Just to make sure, Cole rummaged through the contents of both bags, taking out everything in them and lining them up on the table. The items in the bags took up all the available space.

"Nope, no change of clothes," he announced.

"Mr. Cole," Rita began, her voice trailing off along with her patience.

Cole did his best not to sigh. "You want me to go to the general store and buy some clothes for the twins," he guessed.

"Very good," Rita replied, smiling at him.

"What size do you want me to get for them?" he asked.

"Why don't you get the outfits to fit a three-month-old, just to be on the safe side?" Stacy said, speaking up.

He'd almost forgotten she was there. "Okay," he said gamely. "How many outfits do you want me to buy?" he asked Stacy.

The housekeeper took over. "Three for each should do," Rita told him, adding, "As long as you don't mind doing a lot of washing."

Cole frowned slightly. The idea of having to wash clothes—even tiny ones—didn't warm his heart. "I'll get five," he told Rita.

Rita turned before he could see the smile on her face. "Whatever you say, Mr. Cole," the housekeeper replied.

"Yeah, right." Cole laughed under his breath. "Be back as soon as I can. We should have thought of this earlier, when we were in town," he said to Stacy as he walked out.

"Yes, we should have," Stacy answered, addressing his back.

From Stacy's tone, he didn't know if she was agreeing with him or mocking him. He decided that he was better off not knowing.

"Come," Rita said to her as she cradled Mike in the crook of her arm while picking up a package of disposable diapers with her other hand. "We can change these two in the guest bedroom." She led the way to the other room.

"WHAT ARE YOU doing back in town?" Miss Joan asked sharply when she saw Cole walking through the diner's door.

Accustomed to her prickly manner, Cole came up to the counter. "That's no way to make a customer feel wanted, Miss Joan."

"You're not wanted," Miss Joan informed him. "In case it slipped your mind, you're supposed to be with those babies." Her hazel eyes pinned him with a look. "Where are they?"

"I left them with Rita and Stacy at the ranch," Cole told her. He thought that would please her. He quickly discovered that he was wrong.

"And you ran off?" Miss Joan accused. "Responsibility getting to be too much for you already, boy?" Cole wasn't sure if that was disappointment in her eyes, or if she was just trying to goad him. "Lucky for you your brother didn't feel that way or you, Cody and Cassidy would have been scattered to the four corners of Texas."

"I'm not shirking my responsibility, Miss Joan," Cole assured her. "I just came back to town to get them a change of clothes at the general store. Rita insisted that they were going to need them."

Rather than saying anything about making a mistake, or even that she'd known, in her heart, that he would come through, Miss Joan focused on what his housekeeper had said.

"Of course they will," Miss Joan agreed with feeling. "You can't have those babies in the same clothes day in, day out."

Day in, day out. That sounded much too long a stretch of time to him. He just couldn't think about that now. Instead, he defended his reasoning.

"They're babies, Miss Joan. They just need blankets tucked around them and they've already got those."

Miss Joan just shook her head. "You are going to need a lot of work, boy," she commented with feeling. Her eyes narrowed as she pinned him with a look. "If you came into town for extra clothes, what are you doing here?" she asked. "In case you hadn't noticed, I don't sell baby clothes."

"I just wanted a cup of your hot, bracing coffee before I went back to the ranch," he told her.

"You just wanted to stall before you went back," Miss Joan corrected. "Don't forget, I've known you since you were no taller than the heel on that boot you're wearing. I know how you think. Babies are nothing to be afraid of, Cole," she said, pouring him a tall container to go. "And neither is Stacy," she added in a low voice.

"I'm not afraid," he said defensively. "She made the decision to go her own way eight months ago," he added, lowering his voice so that no one else but Miss Joan could hear.

Miss Joan made no comment. Instead, she placed a lid on the coffee she had just poured and pushed the container toward him.

"Just take your coffee and get back to the ranch— and your responsibilities."

"They're not my responsibilities, Miss Joan," he reminded her.

"Haven't you heard?" Miss Joan asked. "Possession is nine tenths of the law and they're on your property. That makes them yours."

Cole sighed, digging into his pocket. Arguing with Miss Joan about *anything* was futile. "So, what do I owe you?"

Her eyes met his. "Prove me right and we'll call it even," Miss Joan told him. "Now get your tail out of here. Those kids are waiting."

Again, he couldn't argue with her, even if he wanted to. Because somewhere in his heart, he felt that she was right.

HE DRANK THE coffee on the trip back.

When he walked into the ranch house with the extra baby clothes that Rita had sent him out to get, he found his housekeeper and his former girlfriend sitting on the living room sofa, feeding the twins and laughing. Obviously, in the time it had taken him to go to town and back, a lot of bonding had taken place.

"There you are," Rita announced when she saw him come in. "I was beginning to think you decided not to come back."

"I haven't been gone that long," Cole protested. He handed her the bag of clothes he'd bought. "Still don't see why I had to buy these. All they need are their diapers, their undershirts and those blankets they were wrapped up in when I found them in that basket on the doorstep."

"And you are an expert on babies?" Rita asked.

Maybe he wasn't an expert, but he did have some experience. "We've had two here."

Rita frowned at him. "And how much attention did you pay?" she asked.

"Enough," Cole answered defensively.

Rita shook her head and he got the feeling that she was pitying him. Standing up, she handed over Mike to him. "Here, you hold him. I have dinner to finish preparing. See that you do not drop him," she ordered, walking back into the kitchen.

"I like her," Stacy told him as Cole sat down beside her with Mike.

"You would," he answered. And then his curiosity got the better of him. "What were you two laughing about when I walked in?"

"Oh, were we laughing?" Stacy asked innocently. "I hadn't realized."

"Even the twins realized it," he pointed out, still waiting for her to answer his question.

"Just girl talk," she finally answered. "Nothing important."

She wasn't about to say anything more, he thought. For now, he let it go—but he promised himself that he would find out eventually.

Chapter Eight

After parking his truck near the front of the ranch house, Connor remained seated behind the steering wheel for a couple of minutes, gathering his strength together just to make it to the front door.

He felt really drained. He was going to have to get some part-time help, he told himself. Even with Cole's help—which he hadn't had today—there was just too much work on the ranch.

Uttering a deep sigh he opened the driver's side door and got out. Connor recalled that his father had an expression that rather aptly described the way he was feeling as he all but dragged himself up to his front door: he felt as if he had been ridden hard and put away wet.

Of course, the expression more accurately applied to a horse, but Connor felt that, in this case, it also could have just as easily described him.

Walking into the house, the first thing he saw was Cole, pacing the floor with what looked like a doll wrapped up in a blanket in his arms. Connor blinked and realized he was looking at an infant, not a doll.

At least, he assumed it was an infant. He'd heard that

these days they had realistic-looking dolls that did everything except chop wood and herd cattle, so it could still be a doll.

He took a closer look.

It wasn't a doll.

"You know, I could have used a hand today," Connor said, shrugging out of his jacket and letting it fall over the back of the easy chair as he walked past it.

"I'm really sorry about that," Cole said. "But something came up." He nodded at the infant in his arms, then raised his eyes to look at his brother again. "Or maybe I should say *two* somethings came up."

That was when Connor noticed that Cole wasn't alone in the living room. There was a young woman sitting on the sofa.

Stacy Rowe.

She was back—and she was holding another infant in her arms.

Stacy turned around just then to look at him and she smiled in acknowledgment.

"Stacy." Remembering that he was still wearing his hat, Connor took it off as a sign of respect. "I didn't know that you were back in town," he told her. "How are you?"

Rather than answer Connor's question with the all-encompassing word *fine*, because she wasn't really fine, Stacy told Cole's older brother, "I'm well, thank you for asking, Connor."

Connor recalled his brother's phone call earlier today, saying something about finding babies on his doorstep. Because he always took the simpler route if it was opened to him, Connor put two and two together and asked, "Are they yours?" nodding toward the infant she was holding.

Again, rather than give Connor a direct yes or no answer, Stacy replied, "Cole found them on his doorstep today."

Suppressing a weary sigh, he turned his attention back to his brother. "So you still don't know who the mother is," Connor concluded, remembering what his brother had said earlier when he'd called.

Cole shook his head. "No one's come forward to claim them," he said. "The sheriff's going to see what he can find out, and Joe Lone Wolf's going to do a little poking around on the reservation just in case they belong to one of the women there."

Connor filled in the blanks. A desperate young girl finding herself pregnant and alone, taking the only avenue she felt was open to her. It wasn't that unusual a scenario. Still, he hoped that wasn't the case.

"You told Miss Joan about the babies, right?" Connor asked, thinking, the way everyone else in the area did, that if anyone would know who the babies' mother was, it was Miss Joan.

"Right," Cole answered. "She told me that she'd let me know if she heard any talk about someone having recently given birth to twins."

Connor paused beside Stacy, his mind going a mile a minute as he looked at the infant in her arms.

"I think we still have Cassidy's old crib in the attic,"

he said. "We took it down while Devon and the baby were here, but I took it apart and put it back up in the attic. Looks like we need to bring it back down again."

Stacy knew that Connor was nothing if not kind-hearted. All the McCulloughs were. But taking in two extra children—infants at that—was an imposition. She was surprised that he didn't balk at the idea. "So it's okay if they stay here?" she asked.

"They got anyplace else to go?" Connor asked her matter-of-factly.

"No."

"Then I guess that settles that question. They can stay here until their parents turn up or something else can be arranged." Connor turned toward his brother. "Cole, I'm dead tired. Help me bring that crib down. We'll put it together so these kids can have something softer to sleep in than that basket you've got over there." He nodded at the wicker basket that was on the floor near the oversize coffee table.

For a second, Cole looked as if he was at a loss as to what to do with the infant in his arms. Spying the basket his brother had just referred to, he placed Mike in it. He brought it back around and put the basket next to Stacy's feet.

"Okay," he told Connor. "Let's do this."

THEY FOUND THE crib more or less where Connor had put it. It was in four pieces, not counting the springs and the mattress that would eventually rest on the springs once the four sides of the crib were joined together.

It took them three trips each to bring down all the pieces.

Working together, with some slight supervision coming from Rita, who had decided to check on the babies, Connor and Cole put the crib together rather quickly, considering that some of the hardware was missing.

Cole didn't believe in just throwing things together and he wasn't satisfied until he'd tested the crib for sturdiness.

"That looks really strong," Stacy told them once Cole and his brother were finished and had stepped back from their project.

"It would have to be," Cole said. "Cassidy was the last one to use it on a long-term basis and she was always hard on her things—furniture, clothes, you name it."

"She'd shake those bars until she finally found a way to climb out," Connor said, smiling and remembering. "And then she'd make a break for it whenever she could. Dad talked about tying her up for the night. The rest of us knew he was kidding, but that made her even more determined to climb out."

"I'm surprised the crib wasn't in pieces," Stacy commented. "I guess they made things to last twenty-three years ago."

"Our dad made this crib," Connor told her. "Our mother told me that he made it just before I was born and all four of us slept in it until we outgrew it—which, in Cassidy's case, was pretty quick."

He looked at the infant she was still holding. It had

fallen asleep in her arms. "I think because these babies are on the small side, they can both fit in the crib together," he remarked.

"Are you going to leave it right here in the middle of the living room?" Stacy asked skeptically. "Wouldn't everyone, including the twins, be better off if the crib was in that back bedroom that's down here?"

Connor thought the matter over for a moment. "You might have a point. But the other two times we've made use of it this last year, there was always someone to sleep in the same room as the baby. First Devon, and then Cassidy slept in the room with the baby she rescued."

"Well, how about Cole?" Stacy suggested, a smile curving the corners of her mouth for the first time that day as she turned to look at him. "After all, he was the one who found them."

Cole was far from sold on the idea. "Well, I—" he began to demur.

"Are you going to tell me that a man can't do something a woman can do?" Stacy asked. She was clearly challenging him and he knew it.

"Not *can't*," Cole stressed. "But in this case, a woman could do it better." A way out occurred to him. "Stacy, didn't you say you had nowhere to stay?"

"No, I said I was staying at the hotel," Stacy corrected.

"*Because* you had no place to stay," Cole reminded her. He brought up an obvious point. "Your house burned down while you were away so when you came back, you didn't have a place to live."

"I know all that," she said impatiently. She didn't need him to bring up the obvious. She was still having a hard time dealing with that loss as well as the loss of her aunt.

"Instead of staying at the hotel, why don't you stay here?" Connor asked.

She didn't want to stay here because she didn't want to set herself up for any more pain than she'd already gone through. The memory of the way she'd felt over eight months ago, when she'd left Forever, was still fresh enough to not just make her wary, but make her want to keep away from Cole as much as she possibly could.

And how's that working out for you? Stacy mocked herself.

Out loud, she said, "I appreciate the offer, Connor, but I have a job at the hotel. I just got hired today to take over the reception desk."

"We could really use your help here," Connor told her. "And I'd take it as a personal favor if you pitched in," he added.

She felt herself wavering and struggled to remain steadfast. "But I can't just leave Rebecca high and dry like that. I've already postponed starting my job for one day because of the babies—well, I didn't exactly postpone it, Miss Joan told me that she would do it for me." Coming from Miss Joan, it had sounded more like an order than an offer.

"You seem to have a knack for these babies," Connor said, playing on her sympathies. "And in the grand scheme of things, taking care of infants is a lot more important than working a reception desk at a hotel that only has a moderate amount of business most of the months of the year.

"Of course, I can't tell you what to do, but since Cole seems to have brought these lost little souls here, and I have the ranch to run while Cole works both here and at the Healing Ranch, I would *really* take it as a personal favor if you could help out at least part of the time," he stressed. "In exchange, you can stay here for as long as you'd like. You can have your own bedroom and Rita will help with the—they *are* twins, aren't they?" he asked.

"Dr. Dan seemed to think so when we had them checked out at the clinic," Cole told his brother.

That was good enough for Connor. "Twins it is. And Rita can help you take care of them until we get home at night."

Stacy felt as if she was being hemmed in. "I would love to help," she began, "but—"

"You already made plans and your mind is made up," Connor guessed. Resigned, he nodded. "I understand. I have no intentions of forcing you to do something you don't want to do." He took a breath. "I didn't see another car out front besides Cole's when I came home so I'm assuming you came over here with him. He'll take you back," Connor told her.

She rolled it over in her mind. "Yes, he will," Stacy said as she stood up. "He'll take me back so I can explain to Rebecca in person why I won't be able to take the job after all, and so I can pack my things," she added. "I'm going to need a few changes of clothing myself if I'm going to be staying here—for a while."

Connor beamed and took both of her hands in his. "I can't thank you enough," he told Stacy.

Looking up at him, Stacy smiled. "Maybe I should be the one thanking you," she said. "I'd forgotten what it's like here in Forever—with people going the extra mile for each other, even when they don't have to."

"I can't pay you much, but—" Connor began.

She stopped him before he got any further. "No, it's all right. I'm sure this is just going to be temporary—and Aunt Kate did leave me a little in her will, so I'm not exactly hurting for money yet." She could see he was about to protest and she knew what he was going to say. "I took the job at the hotel mainly to keep busy, not because I was destitute."

Connor seemed to hardly hear the second half of her statement.

"My lord, I forgot all about your aunt's passing." Sympathy flashed through his eyes. "I am really sorry to hear about that. Your aunt was a fine lady."

Stacy nodded. "Aunt Kate had a good life. And she got to see Europe the way she always wanted to," she pointed out.

The import of her own words hit her for the first time. Until just now, she had thought of the last eight months as her aunt rescuing her and taking her away from her source of pain, but now she realized that she had actually rendered a service to her aunt, as well. For as long as she could remember, Aunt Kate had always talked about traveling someday. By giving her aunt a reason to take her away, she had inadvertently provided that "someday" for Aunt Kate to finally see Europe.

Everything happened for a reason, Stacy remembered her mother used to say. She supposed that, in this case, she had ultimately done good for her aunt by letting the woman whisk her away from Forever.

"All right then," Connor was saying. "Cole, why don't you take Stacy back to the hotel so she can collect her things and make her peace with Rebecca? Meanwhile," he went on, turning toward the twins, who were now comfortably nestled in the crib he and Cole had put together, "I'll wash the dust off and roll up my sleeves so I can take care of these two until you get back."

"Dinner will be ready in another hour, hour and a half," Rita called out to Cole and Stacy, as if on cue, despite the fact that she wasn't in the room. "Make sure you are back from the town by then, Mr. Cole. Miss Stacy," she added pointedly.

From the housekeeper's tone of voice, Stacy got the impression that it wasn't a suggestion on the woman's part—it was an order.

Taking her arm, Cole guided Stacy out the door and then to his truck.

Seated, she eyed him quizzically as Cole got in on the driver's side.

"I think we'd better get a move on if we're going to be back in time," he told her, starting up his truck.

She buckled up. "You make it sound like Rita rules the roost around here."

Cole laughed under his breath. "Let's just say I've learned not to make her unhappy. Connor's her boss, but as for the rest of us, I think, given her age, she kind of sees us like her kids. Trust me, staying on the right side of that lady has its advantages," he told her with feeling.

"The rest of you," Stacy repeated. Aware that things might have changed while she'd been gone, she was trying to get a handle on the way things were. "Then Cody and Cassidy still live on the ranch?"

"Not anymore," he told her. "But they come by often enough, along with their spouses and the kids."

"Spouses," she echoed as if she was having trouble absorbing the word and what it meant, at least in one case. "You mean that Cassidy got married?"

He saw the stunned expression on her face. He'd felt the same way at the time.

"That's right. You weren't here for that." Cole grinned broadly, relishing being able to reveal the details to her. "And you're never going to guess who she married."

Stacy had no idea who her friend had married. But she was fairly certain about one thing. "Well, I know she didn't marry Will Laredo," Stacy began.

The grin on Cole's face widened, stopped her dead. "Wrong."

Stacy's eyes widened. She looked at him, stunned. "You're kidding."

Enjoying this, Cole shook his head.

"Cassidy married Will? Really? But those two couldn't be in the same room without verbally slicing each other to ribbons," Stacy recalled.

Cole laughed. "I think they got over that."

Stacy looked at him, allowing herself to *really* look. She'd forgotten how much she'd missed seeing that grin and hearing that laugh.

These last months, Stacy had tried with all her heart to put that behind her. But she'd been in town less than two days and it was flooding back with a vengeance.

If she had a lick of sense, she'd run for the hills the first opportunity she had, Stacy told herself.

Somehow, she had a feeling that wasn't going to happen.

Chapter Nine

Cole pulled his truck into the near-empty parking lot and turned off his engine. "I can wait in the truck if you'd rather talk to Rebecca alone," he offered.

Was he saying he didn't want to go in with her, afraid that people might get the idea that they were back together again? Or was there something else going on? Stacy decided to treat the matter lightly for the time being.

"Is that your way of getting out of carrying down my suitcases?" she asked.

"No, I can still bring those down to the truck. I just thought you'd feel less awkward talking to Rebecca if I wasn't standing right there."

Cole appeared slightly insulted, she thought. If she was going to cast any sort of aspersions in him, she wouldn't waste her breath doing it about something so trivial. Everyone knew the man was the total opposite of lazy.

"I was only kidding about the suitcases," she said. "And as for feeling awkward with you there, talking to Rebecca has nothing to do with it."

Cole cut through the rhetoric and got to the heart of her meaning. "In other words, you'd feel awkward with me around no matter what."

Stacy was *not* in the mood for an argument and waved away his words. "I'll work it out," she said.

They were in the parking lot behind the hotel—Cole had driven more quickly than she'd anticipated—and rather than go round and round about this latest point with him, Stacy just got out of the truck. Without the twins to focus on or having anyone else to serve as a buffer between them, the feeling of awkwardness when they were near each other had returned—in spades.

Closing her door, Stacy told him, "Come inside or stay in the truck. It's all the same to me."

He didn't even have to think about it. "Then I'll come in," Cole responded. He got out and closed the door behind him.

They found Rebecca behind the reception desk, typing on the computer's keyboard. Looking up, the moment she saw Stacy, Rebecca's face dissolved into a wreath of smiles. "I didn't think I'd see you until tomorrow morning," the woman said. She started to come around the desk.

"About that—" Stacy began.

Rebecca stopped where she was. "Wait, I know that tone of voice. You've changed your mind." It wasn't a question.

Stacy wished she didn't feel guilty. Taking the job had been a spur-of-the-moment thing, at best, but that didn't make letting the older woman down any easier.

"Something's come up," Stacy began, trying to edge her way into the explanation.

Rebecca's brown eyes washed over Cole. "Yes, I see that."

For a split second, Rebecca's comment caught her off guard. "What?" The next moment, she realized what the hotel manager was thinking. Stacy quickly tried to set the woman straight. "Oh, no, it's not what you think. I just agreed to help take care of a couple of twins."

Rebecca looked at her in surprise. "You don't strike me as the nanny type."

"That's because I'm not," Stacy answered. "I'm just helping out a friend for a few days—maybe a week or so," Stacy amended. "In any case, I need to check out. If you could have my bill ready when I come back down-stairs, that would be great," Stacy requested.

"Certainly," Rebecca agreed. "Sorry to see you go, Stacy—on both counts."

"Thank you. I hope you find somebody to take over the front desk," Stacy told her as she walked toward the elevator.

"Not as quickly as I found you," Rebecca called after her.

"I feel guilty," Stacy murmured, getting on the el-evator.

The comment hit Cole the wrong way. He bit back the response that rose to his lips. Stacy felt guilty about telling the hotel manager she wasn't taking the job she'd been hired for, but she hadn't given any indication that she felt guilty about just taking off without a word to him the way she had eight months ago.

Cole told himself there was no point in getting angry, but her comment still felt like having salt poured on his wound.

He decided it was best if he didn't say anything to her—about *anything*—for now.

At least, not until he cooled off.

Following her into her hotel room, he waited for Stacy to pack her things. When she was finished and had snapped the locks into place, he took the two suitcases off the bed. Heading toward the door, Cole stood waiting until she exited, then followed her out.

He continued to maintain his silence as he rode down the elevator with her. When they got out to the main floor, he walked out the entrance and took the suitcases to his truck. After loading them into the back, he got in on the driver's side and waited until Stacy took care of her bill at the front desk.

It took her longer than he anticipated, but he said nothing when she finally came out to his truck.

He was giving her the silent treatment, Stacy thought when she finally got into the passenger seat and buckled her seat belt. For the life of her, she had no idea why, or what had changed in the last hour.

If anything, he should be telling her how grateful he was that she had agreed to help out. After all, these babies had been left on his doorstep, not Connor's, and that made them his responsibility. Which actually meant that she was going out of her way to help *him* with them, not Connor.

But then, she didn't know Cole the way she thought she did. There was a time when she would have sworn she knew every thought that entered his head. That was before he'd ridden roughshod over her heart the way he had, completely abandoning her without a second thought.

She supposed that it was lucky for these babies that he'd grown up a bit.

Three minutes into the trip back, the silence was really getting to her.

Because she was not about to ask Cole what was wrong—since that would have given him the impression that she cared—Stacey reached over and turned on the radio.

A popular country singer had only managed to utter the first three words of his song before Cole reached for the dial and, with one quick movement of his wrist, shut the radio off.

"I was listening to that," Stacy protested indignantly.

Cole kept his hand over the dial, stopping her from turning the radio back on. The whole situation had started him thinking. He could come up with only one reason she'd left town and why she was back now, volunteering to help care for the infants he'd "found" on the doorstep.

"Are they yours?"

"What?" she cried sharply, staring at Cole. He couldn't be asking her what she thought he was asking.

"The twins," he specified. "Are they yours? Did you leave them on my doorstep—on the bunkhouse door-step?" he clarified.

Her eyes flashed as she looked at him. "We've already had this discussion. I don't know how bad your memory is, but I answered that question for you and the answer was—and still *is*—no, they are *not* mine," she underscored.

Blowing out a breath, struggling to rein in her temper, she glared at him. Like it or not, she was still able to read him.

"You don't believe me, do you?" Cole didn't answer her. It was getting harder for her to hold on to her temper. "Do you think that little of me that you believe I'd just leave two helpless infants crammed in a basket on a doorstep?" she demanded heatedly.

"My doorstep."

That did it. "I didn't know you even *had* a damn doorstep other than at the ranch until this happened so, no, it wasn't me. They're not mine—get over yourself, Cole."

"I can get over myself with no trouble at all," Cole assured her. And then, in what he realized was a moment of weakness, he told her, "What I can't seem to get over is you."

Did he honestly think she was going to believe that? Maybe she never really knew him at all, she thought sadly. "I stopped believing in Santa Claus a long time ago, Cole. So please stop trying to snow me."

"You don't believe me." Served him right for saying anything to her, he upbraided himself.

"No," she told him flatly. "I don't."

He spared her one piercing glance, then looked straight ahead at the flat terrain. "Yeah, well, I don't believe me, either, but there it is." And then he couldn't help throwing in, "Even though you left without a single word of explanation—"

Was he delusional? Or was he just trying to make her doubt herself? "I didn't think I needed to explain anything, considering that *you* were the one who decided to bail out."

"I didn't bail out," he insisted. "I just needed time to think."

"Yeah, think about how to bail out," she retorted angrily. They'd made love and after what she'd thought was the most wonderful night of her life, he'd vanished on her. "Face it, you got what you wanted, so the bloom was off the rose and you wanted to explore other fields."

The more he talked to her, the more confused he became.

"What the hell are you talking about?" Cole demanded. "This is Forever, population *small*. There *are* no other fields."

He was almost convincing, she thought. But she'd lived through it, lived through the humiliation of having him take off the way he had, without a backward glance. Well, two could play that game, and thanks to Aunt Kate, she had.

"Denial is only a good weapon when you're on a diet

and find yourself stranded in a bakery. In your case, denial is definitely not good—especially for your soul."

"Let's stop right here," Cole warned her, "before one of us says something we can't take back. It's best for everyone all around if we just focus on those two babies back at the ranch who need to be reunited with their mother."

She didn't want to argue, and if she remained around him, they were bound to argue. "Maybe I can be more useful if I volunteer to help the sheriff look for her."

"Maybe," Cole allowed. "It's an option you can look into in the morning. Right now, if I don't bring you back in time for dinner, neither one of us might live to see morning."

He almost succeeded in making her laugh. "Rita can't be *that* fierce."

"Let's put it this way. In our house, nobody has ever tried to call her bluff. Besides, she cooks like an angel," he told her. "And I don't know about you, but I'm really getting kind of hungry."

She didn't want to admit it, but now that Cole had mentioned it, she was rather hungry herself. "Just drive," she told him, waving her hand toward the road in front of them, and let it go at that.

CONNOR APPEARED GENUINELY relieved when he saw Stacy walk in with his brother.

"I was afraid you might have changed your mind," he told her. "I don't mind admitting that I think I'm out of my depth here." He nodded at the infants currently in the crib. "Feeding two of these is a lot harder than just feeding one," he told his new houseguest. "When Devon was here with her newborn, we all took turns helping out, but she did most of the heavy lifting, so to speak. And then when Cassidy rescued that baby and brought her here, Rita had started to work for us. And there was also Will to pitch in."

"Will," Stacy echoed. "Laredo?" She said the rancher's last name just to be sure they were talking about the same man. "I don't think I can picture him helping with a baby."

Cole laughed. "He kind of felt it was his duty because—Cassidy didn't like letting anyone know this at the time—Will actually rescued Cassidy rescuing the baby."

"They were in the middle of a flash flood and the current got pretty strong pretty fast, according to the locals. If it hadn't been for Will, Cassidy and the baby might have both been swept away," Connor told her. "My point is that there was always just one baby to a whole bunch of us. Now there're two babies, and our numbers have decreased considerably."

When she'd walked in, Stacy had been having serious second thoughts about what she was signing on for—even if it turned out to be only for a short while. But listening to Connor just now, she'd had another change of heart. As annoyed as she kept getting with Cole, she couldn't, in all good conscience, bring herself to just leave Connor high and dry.

"Well, if it helps any," she told Connor, "consider those numbers to have increased by one. I officially terminated my job at the hotel and I'm here to help until the sheriff locates their mother."

"Dinner is ready," Rita announced, walking into the living room. "Eat," she ordered, waving the three people into the dining room. "I will take care of the babies. That means you, too," she told Stacy when the latter made no move to leave the room.

And, just like that, Stacy found herself an unofficial member of the family—at least for the time being.

THE FIRST COUPLE of days on the ranch seemed to run together for Stacy, turning into an endless stream of feedings and diaperings with occasional fitful snatches of sleep. The twins seemed to take turns being awake, never sleeping at the same time.

Initially, trying to keep up with them felt like an exercise in futility to Stacy until the housekeeper took over, ordering her to her room.

"You sleep, I will take care of the babies," she told her.

"No, that's all right, Rita," Stacy protested, sounding a little exhausted around the edges. "You have work to do."

"Yes," the woman agreed, leveling a penetrating gaze directly at Stacy. "And you are making it hard for me to do it." With one baby tucked into the crook of her arm, Rita pointed to the ground floor bedroom, next to the twins' room, that had been set aside to act as Stacy's. "Now go lie down and get some rest before Mr. Cole accuses me of letting you run yourself into the ground."

It wasn't in her to argue for longer than half a moment, but she couldn't leave without correcting Rita's obvious mistake. "You mean Mr. Connor."

"No," Rita countered, "I mean Mr. Cole. Mr. Cole wanted me to keep an eye on you and make sure you get your rest," the housekeeper told her. "He said that if I didn't watch you, you would try to do too much and forget about taking care of yourself. Nobody wants to see you getting sick."

Stacy frowned. That didn't make any sense. She and Cole weren't exactly on the best of terms after that ride back from the hotel. "Are you sure you're not talking about Mr. Connor?"

"I am sure," Rita told her. "They do not look alike. And besides, Mr. Connor is a good man, but he is not the one who is in love with you."

The housekeeper had to be imagining things. "Well, I have news for you, Rita. Neither is Mr. Cole," Stacy assured her. "And whatever he might have told you—" she began, positive that the woman had misunderstood something or taken it out of its context, but she never got the chance.

"He did not tell me anything, Miss Stacy," the housekeeper said with finality. "He did not have to. I can see it in his eyes."

There was no arguing with the woman, Stacy thought, giving up. Rita was just like Miss Joan, stubborn to the very end.

Stacy sighed. "I think I'll take that nap now," she told the woman, surrendering.

Rita smiled. "That is a very good idea. And don't worry about the little ones, they will be in good hands."

It must be nice, Stacy thought as she went into the small bedroom, to be so confident. The only time she had been that confident about something, she turned out to be wrong.

Even if Rita was determined to argue that point.

But Rita was wrong even if she didn't know it.

Stacy put her head down on the pillow and was sound asleep before she could complete her thought.

Chapter Ten

It was dark when she woke up.

And there was a blanket draped over her.

Stacy didn't remember pulling a blanket over herself. She barely remembered lying down. What she did remember was that she'd intended to sleep for no more than twenty minutes—if that much.

The sun had been coming into her room when she lay down. It was gone now. This had to be way past twenty minutes.

Sitting up, she pulled the blanket off and placed it on the edge of the bed. She became aware of people talking to each other. And laughing.

Stacy got off the bed and walked to the door. Opening it allowed not just the living room light and the laughter to enter, but the feeling of warmth, as well. Both Connor and Cole were home and each of them was holding one of the twins. She couldn't help thinking how totally natural that looked.

"I'm sorry," Connor said the moment he saw her coming into the living room. "We were making too much noise and woke you up."

"Don't apologize," she told him. "I wasn't supposed to sleep this long." She looked around for a clock. "What time is it?"

"Just a little after six," Cole answered.

"Six?" Stacy echoed incredulously. "It was just one o'clock when I lay down. I was only supposed to nap for a few minutes," she said, totally distressed.

"You were supposed to nap for as long as you needed to," Cole told her. You've been up for practically the last forty-eight hours. It was bound to catch up with you," he pointed out.

Rita was in the room, as well, and she turned her attention toward the housekeeper. "I'm sorry, Rita," she apologized. "I didn't mean to leave you with all this work."

"You did not leave me with anything," the older woman informed her. "I was the one who told you to get some sleep," she reminded Stacy. "You were more tired than you knew. Mr. Connor and Mr. Cole each took turns dropping by during the day so I was not alone the whole time. And they have both been here since five o'clock. The babies have been angels," the housekeeper added, then told her, "You are up just in time for dinner."

"Dinner? Didn't you already serve dinner?" she asked. Dinner was on the table like clockwork at five every night. Why had the woman postponed serving it?

"Tonight, Rita decided to wait," Cole told her.

She couldn't help wondering if it was Rita who'd made the decision or if Connor and Cole had told the housekeeper to hold the meal until she woke up. She slanted a glance at Rita. The housekeeper was beginning to seem more like a benevolent dictator than a tyrant to her.

"Did you come in and cover me when I was asleep?" Stacy asked the woman as she followed Rita to the dining room.

Rita paused for a moment to turn and look at her. "You are a grown woman. You can cover yourself if you feel the need. Besides, I was busy taking care of the babies. Sit," she ordered, then went into the kitchen to bring in the meal she had prepared.

Connor and Cole placed the drowsy twins back in the crib and came to the dining room behind her.

Stacy looked over at the McCullough brothers who were taking their seats at the table, Connor at its head and Cole across from her.

Connor smiled as he observed, "You look better now, Stacy. I don't mind admitting that I was getting worried about you."

Cole avoided making eye contact with her. She suspected she knew why.

"It was you, wasn't it?" she asked him. "You came in and covered me. Why didn't you wake me up?"

"Because you looked so peaceful." Not to mention beautiful, he thought, looking at the fiery redhead. And then Cole stopped abruptly. "That was a trick, wasn't it?"

"I don't know what you mean," Stacy answered innocently.

He would have denied being the one who covered her if Stacy hadn't distracted him by asking why he hadn't woken her up. Blue eyes met blue. "I don't remember you being devious."

Stacy smiled, tossing her head and sending waves of red swinging about her face. "I prefer to think of it as resourceful—and that's something I've had to become. Resourceful, not devious," she clarified.

The strong aroma of fried chicken preceded Rita as she came in carrying a large heaping platter of legs and breasts. The housekeeper placed it in the middle of the table.

"That smells heavenly," Stacy told the woman with deep appreciation.

Rita beamed. "I know. Mashed potatoes and green beans are coming," she announced.

Stacy began to get up. "Let me help you with that."

Rita pushed the chair back in under her. For a small lady, the housekeeper was surprisingly strong.

"You sit," she ordered. Turning to Cole, she instructed, "You, come with me."

"Yes, ma'am," he replied with a grin.

Watching Cole get up and follow Rita, Stacy felt her heart being tugged. His grin had the same effect on her now that it always used to have—before things went so wrong.

If she wasn't careful, Stacy silently warned herself, she was going to fall into the same trap she had all those months ago. She was supposed to learn from her mistakes, not make them all over again.

Coming back into the dining room, Cole placed the large bowl of warm mashed potatoes right next to her.

"I remember you were partial to mashed potatoes," he told her.

Stacy had no idea why that should have touched her. But it did. He had remembered a small, inconsequential detail about her that made no difference in the grand scheme of things—but it did to her. And he had remembered.

"There is gravy," Rita said, putting the gravy bowl right next to the potatoes. Retreating, she went to bring in the green beans. When she returned, the housekeeper placed the vegetables beside the fried chicken. "Now eat," she dictated, declaring, "Everything is already getting cold."

A small wail was heard from the living room. Reacting in unison, Connor and Cole both began to rise.

"I said eat," Rita reminded them in a firmer voice. "I will take care of the babies." Her eyes swept over the threesome seated at the table. "I expect to see clean plates when I come back."

Stacy smiled to herself. "Definitely a benevolent dictator," she said after the woman had left the dining room.

"I'm beginning to think that she's actually Miss Joan, wearing a wig," Cole said.

"No, she's too short," Connor pointed out. "But somewhere, way back a couple of generations ago, those two had to have shared the same forebearers."

No sooner had they finished discussing the similarities of the two women's approaches to the people around them than Rita walked back into the room with one twin in her arms.

"I need to get a bottle," she told them matter-of-factly. On her way to the kitchen, the housekeeper still paused to see if the people she technically worked for were eating as she had told them to. "How is everything?" she asked.

From her tone it was clear that she expected only to hear good things.

Stacy spoke up first. There was no hesitation in her voice when she said, "Perfect."

"You've outdone yourself, Rita," Connor said, adding his voice to Stacy's.

"Fried chicken's a little dry," Cole deadpanned. And then he couldn't keep it back any longer and laughed. "Just kidding."

Rita's dark eyes narrowed as she gave Cole a piercing stare.

"You are lucky that my hands are busy with this baby right now, or you would learn that there is nothing funny about saying something insulting about my cooking that is not true."

Cole backed off immediately. "Everyone knows you couldn't ruin anything you made if you tried, Rita," Cole told her, turning his charm up full volume. He gave her a soulful look. "Am I forgiven?"

Stacy fully expected the woman to relent, succumb to Cole's charm and say yes.

Instead, she heard Rita tell him, "I do not forgive

so easily. I will be keeping my eye on you, Mr. Cole," she warned.

"Then I'll just have to do something special," Cole teased.

In response, Rita's expression only grew darker. Stacy couldn't tell if the woman was only pretending to be annoyed, or if her humor was on a completely different wavelength than Cole's.

Cole appealed to his older brother. "You're her favorite. Tell her I was only kidding."

"Don't look at me," Connor said, pretending to want nothing to do with the joke that had fallen so completely flat on its face. "I was busy eating and enjoying this wonderful meal that Rita made for us. And by the way, the chicken, Rita," he said, looking at the housekeeper, "is fantastic."

"Fantastic," Cole echoed with enthusiasm.

"You had your chance," was all Rita said to Cole as she walked into the kitchen with the baby.

"Maybe you shouldn't tease her like that," Stacy told Cole.

Now that the housekeeper was in the other room, Cole appeared totally unfazed. "Rita knows that I don't mean anything by it. It's a way for everybody to blow off some steam. We'd all go through fire for that lady and she would readily do the same for all of us. It's a given," he told Stacy.

Stacy wasn't a hundred percent convinced. "I don't know. Rita looked pretty annoyed to me just now."

Stacy fell silent as Rita returned to the dining room.

Mike was tucked into the crook of her arm and she fed him with the warmed bottle. She tossed an icy glance in Cole's direction.

"Only one piece of pie for you tonight," she decreed as she continued walking to the living room.

Rita was kidding, Stacy thought. The slight smile at the corners of the woman's thin mouth right before she walked out gave her away.

"I guess she does realize that you're kidding," Stacy said. "This is going to take some getting used to."

It was only after she'd said it that she understood what that sounded like—like she intended to stay longer than just a few days or, at most, another week looking after the babies until their mother could be tracked down or came forward on her own.

From the smile she saw on Connor's lips, that was exactly what he was thinking. If she said anything in protest, that would only make things worse, so she decided to let the whole thing go.

Instead, she asked, "Anyone hear anything from the sheriff about the babies' mother? Has he got any leads yet?"

Cole laughed at the way she'd worded her question. "This isn't exactly a detective novel, Stacy. And I think if the sheriff had any *leads*, he would have either sent Cody to the ranch to tell us or come himself. Looks like the kids' mother is going to remain a mystery for at least a while longer."

"You don't think that anything happened to her, do

you?" Stacy asked as she suddenly thought of that possibility.

"Exactly what do you mean by 'happened'?" Cole asked.

She resisted saying more, but she supposed that there was no getting away from the possibility of that being one of the scenarios.

Even so, the words were hard for her to utter. "You know, like, she died."

"You mean right after leaving them on my doorstep?" Cole asked.

This was gruesome, but she was the one who had brought it up, so she continued advancing the theory. "I know that sounds like a coincidence, but coincidences *do* happen sometimes."

"This is a very small town, Stacy," Connor gently reminded her. "Unless the twins' mother was buried in a rock slide without a trace, if someone dies in or near Forever, Rick would know about it."

"All right, let's look at this whole thing from a different angle," Stacy suggested.

"Such as?" Cole asked, unclear as to where she wanted to go with this.

"Such as the twins' mother deliberately *picked* you to leave her babies with," Stacy told him.

He still didn't understand. "What are you saying?" Cole asked.

"I'm saying that the easiest thing for the twins' mother to do might have been to leave the babies on the clinic doorstep. Or on Miss Joan's doorstep, for that matter. But, instead, their mother left them on *your* doorstep. She *picked* you, not anyone else," Stacy stressed.

Cole was definitely not ready to go with that theory. "Maybe she just picked the first doorstep she came to."

Stacy shook her head. "The Healing Ranch is out of the way. And the bunkhouse is even *more* out of the way than that. No, I think she picked you on purpose." The more she considered the matter, the more Stacy was sure that she was on to something. "I'm not saying the twins are yours. I'm just asking if you know anyone who was, well, in the family way recently? Someone you were nice to?"

The look he gave Stacy said she had to be kidding. "I spend most of the week here, working with Connor, and usually a couple of days and nights at the Healing Ranch, which is dedicated to helping troubled boys, so, no, I haven't noticed anyone in the *family way* in the last few weeks—or before then, either," Cole told her.

Stacy sighed. So much for that idea. "So then you haven't noticed anybody who looked as if they were expecting a baby?"

"No, *nobody*," Cole answered, just in case there was any room for doubt.

"Why don't we just leave this up to the professionals?" Connor suggested, specifying, "Rick, Cody and Joe."

Stacy sighed. "I guess we don't have any other choice."

"Don't sound so depressed about it, Stacy," Connor

told her. "Forever might be a small town, but Rick's not a hayseed and he's been at this for some time now.

"And you're forgetting about the reservation. If their mother is still out there, they'll find her. Now let's do justice to Rita's dinner or she just might decide not to let *any* of us have dessert."

That sounded a little over the top, considering that the woman did work for him. "You're kidding, right?" Stacy asked.

"When it comes to Rita," Connor answered, "I've learned not to kid."

Stacy couldn't tell if he was serious or not. She decided not to question him. They had bigger concerns right now.

"You know," Cole said, thinking, "what you said isn't half bad."

Stacy looked at him a little uncertainly. "You mean about someone deliberately leaving the babies so that you'd be the one to find them?"

"Yeah. It doesn't have to be someone I know, just someone who knows me."

"Because you're so wonderful?" Had he gotten a swelled head after all? It occurred to her that he might have changed a lot in the last eight months.

"No, because whoever their mother is, she knows I wouldn't let anything happen to those babies and I'd make sure they were safe."

Much as she hated to admit it, Stacy knew he had hit the nail on the head. And, if she was being honest, she was rather relieved that the babies weren't Cole's—

even though she told herself that wasn't supposed to matter to her.

But it did.

Chapter Eleven

Stacy frowned slightly to herself as she was feeding Mikey. Mikey was more restless than his twin, but that wasn't why she was frowning.

Almost two weeks had gone by and there was still no sign of the twins' mother. Stacy found that rather disturbing and upsetting. Primarily for the twins, because abandonment like that brought issues with it down the line.

However, on a personal level, she found herself hoping that their mother would take a little longer coming forward. She was really beginning to enjoy taking care of the infants, who seemed to be growing daily right in front of her eyes.

Maybe she felt this way because she told herself that this was just temporary, that she'd have to give them up to their mother soon. Not only was she enjoying every minute she was spending with Kate and Mike, but she kept finding new things to enjoy about them.

Like bath time.

Initially, Stacy had been afraid to attempt to bathe either twin and had just used a washcloth to clean them.

It was Cole, not Connor or Rita, who showed her how to properly bathe the twins. He'd helped her get over her fear of somehow inadvertently allowing one of the twins to slip beneath the water and drown.

"There's really nothing to it," Cole told her. "You just make sure you support the baby's head by resting it in the crook of your arm and you use your other hand to wash the baby. You take a washcloth that you've soaped up, rub it along that little body and then you rinse the baby off with the water in the little tub."

"Little tub?" Stacy repeated.

"Yes. I brought it down from the attic last night," Cole told her, then added, "Cassidy left it behind when she married Will and moved to his ranch."

"Why not just use the kitchen sink?" Stacy asked. She knew that Connor and Cole had done some renovations to the house, including replacing the old sink that had been there for decades. "It certainly seems big enough, at least when the twins are this size."

"The tub's softer," Cole told her. "It's easier on their little bottoms. Miss Joan took up a collection for the baby that Cassidy rescued the same way she did when Devon had hers. Being Miss Joan, she'll probably do the same for these two if their mother doesn't show up," he said, nodding at the twins, who were both in the crib they shared. "The woman's got a heart of gold even if at times it seems like she has a tongue that can cut a person in half at ten paces."

Stacy laughed. "That's a pretty accurate description of Miss Joan. I guess that's what makes her so interesting."

"She is that," he agreed. "No doubt about it." And then he looked at Stacy. "All right, enough talking. Are you ready to do this?"

"You mean give the twins a bath with you?" She actually felt butterflies fluttering in her stomach, but she did her best to ignore that.

"More like you give the bath and I'll be there if you need me," Cole corrected. "Too many arms in the tub might get in the way," he explained.

She supposed he had a point, although she wished it was his arms in the tub, not hers—at least, this time around.

"Sure, I can do this," Stacy said, only because saying she couldn't, or would rather that he do it, made her sound like she was afraid, and she refused to come off that way—even if it was true.

"Yes, you can," he agreed quietly, his eyes meeting hers.

He was just encouraging her, Cole told himself. It had nothing to do with the growing feelings he was trying to deny.

Cole fetched the tub and placed it on the spacious kitchen counter. "Okay," he told Stacy, stepping back. "It's all yours."

She filled the small rubber tub halfway with lukewarm water, making sure she had soap and washcloths handy. "It's ready."

Cole nodded and went to her room, where they'd

moved the crib a few days ago. "Looks like you're up first, Mikey," he said. He swiftly took off the baby's shirt and unfastened the diaper's tabs for easy removal, then holding him, quickly brought the infant into the kitchen. "He's all yours," he told Stacy.

Taking Mikey, she positioned him in the crook of her arm, just the way Cole had told her. Then, before immersing Mikey in the tub, she looked at Cole and asked, "You're not leaving, are you?"

Cole smiled reassuringly at her. "I'm going to be right here. Because bath time's fun, isn't it, Mikey?" he asked the baby.

He splashed the little boy ever so lightly, just enough to get a response, but not enough to frighten him or make the woman who was trying to bathe him nervous.

Stacy felt as if time had stood still as she gently lathered the infant's body then rinsed away the soap film on it.

"I guess I'm finished," Stacy said several minutes later, glancing at Cole to see if he thought she'd missed anything.

"Let's see, lather, wash, rinse—yes, you're done," he agreed. "Why don't you take this big boy out of the tub and I'll wrap a towel around him, and then you can dry him off?"

"Sounds good."

Within moments, Cole had a large, fluffy towel wrapped loosely around the baby and she was patting him dry.

"We did it," she declared with a note of triumph a

few minutes later. This was just a minor thing, but she still felt really good about the accomplishment. "I guess we make a pretty good team," she told Cole happily.

Their eyes met over the infant's head and Cole felt an all-too-familiar pull. One he hadn't felt since Stacy had left his life. He'd almost forgotten the swirling warmth that accompanied that feeling.

"I guess we do," Cole answered.

For a split second, he struggled with the strong urge to kiss Stacy. Just to kiss her, to reconnect with this woman he had once felt so strongly about.

But just then, Rita walked in, scattering the moment as she surveyed the kitchen.

"Are you going to be finished soon?" she asked, looking from Cole to the woman holding the baby. "I need my kitchen."

"One twin down," Cole told her, "one to go."

"All right," Rita said. "But don't take all day."

"You heard the lady," Stacy said, handing over Mike to him. "Bring me Katie."

"I'll just get him dressed and be right back with twin number two," Cole told her, hurrying out of the room.

It went faster this time. Stacy didn't know if it was because she felt a little more confident about what she was doing after having bathed Mikey, or if it was because she knew Rita wanted to take the kitchen over and she didn't want to keep the housekeeper waiting indefinitely.

"You're getting really good at this," Cole told her as he wrapped a dripping Katie up in another soft white towel.

His praise pleased her and Stacy smiled in response. "Piece of cake," she said, trying to sound blasé. But in her heart, she was really grateful for his kind words.

Careful, Stace, you don't want to risk going down that path again. He just gave you an offhanded compliment. It wasn't a declaration of love. Besides, you know where a declaration of love leads you—nowhere.

She had to remember that this was first and foremost a favor to Connor. She was also doing this to make sure that the twins didn't wind up getting shipped off to social services. There was no other reason for her to be here, Stacy told herself. She *had* to remember that and focus all her attention on the twins, not on a man who had disappointed her and broken her heart.

Not unless she wanted to endure a repeat performance—which she didn't.

But it was hard to look at Cole in such a negative light. Especially when every time they interacted, she was seeing him at his best. Seeing him being so good with the twins.

The solution to that was not to interact with him, Stacy knew that. However, that was much easier said than done because, although Cole worked hard and was away from the house a good part of each day, somehow it felt to her that he was there a great deal more than he was.

ANOTHER WEEK PASSED and Stacy found that life had arranged itself into an amicable routine for her. Most important of all, although it somehow seemed to happen without her realizing it, she really had become part of a family unit.

Not since her parents died had she been with a family. Feeling so close to the McCulloughs didn't mean that she loved her Aunt Kate any less. Aunt Kate had been a vital part of her life both before her parents had died and after.

But Kate had been only one person. What Stacy found with the McCulloughs was the same thing that she'd found when she'd first been adopted. People to depend on—who also depended on her. People who cared and whom she was slowly but surely finding herself caring about.

Try as she might to resist and talk herself out of it, it was happening. Happening because she knew that part of her needed this, needed to feel as if she was part of a thriving unit.

During that third week, Connor and Cole had moved the twins' crib upstairs to Cassidy's old room. Meanwhile, Stacy had been moved into Cody's old bedroom, which was next to the twins' new room. That way, she could get some much-needed rest at night but still be able to hear the twins if one of them cried.

The move to the new quarters did something else, as well. It made the situation begin to feel permanent, and she knew she couldn't allow herself to get used to that, because despite appearances to the contrary, this *wasn't* permanent. These babies had a mother out there somewhere. A mother who, once she came back to her senses, would rush to reclaim the twins.

And, Stacy told herself, *she* had a life out there, as well. A life that had nothing to do with the McCullough family.

Or with Cole.

She kept reminding herself of that, but she found that it took more and more effort on her part to hang on to that thought.

FEELING RESTLESS ONE EVENING, Stacy went outside after dinner and after the twins had been put down for—she hoped—longer naps than they'd been taking up to this point.

After checking with Rita to see if the housekeeper needed any help with the dishes—and being summarily turned down—Stacy slipped out the front door to get a little air. She had gone out alone, but it wasn't long before she had company.

She'd expected that Connor would come out to make sure she was all right—he was like that. She was beginning to think of him as her own big brother, and since she was an only child, it was a nice feeling.

But instead, when she turned around, she found herself looking up at Cole.

Suddenly, she felt her blood rushing through her veins at a speed that would have made a flash flood envious.

Damn it, what's wrong with you? Stacy scolded herself for being so juvenile. *He's just coming out for some air, same as you.*

"Are you all right out here?" Cole asked.

Was it her imagination, or was he standing too close? It was a cold night, but she was far from that at the moment. She felt warm.

"I'm fine," Stacy told him. "Why?"

Cole shrugged. Maybe he shouldn't have followed her out here. He thought about turning around and going back in. But it was as if his feet were glued to the ground. He wasn't going anywhere.

"Well," he answered, "it's kind of cold tonight and you went out without a jacket or anything. I thought you might have forgotten to take it with you."

She struggled to work up some resentment over the fact that he was treating her like a child—but she couldn't quite do it.

Still, she had to say something. She didn't want him thinking of her as some hapless adolescent. "I think you've been taking care of the twins too long. I don't need looking after."

"Humor me," he told her. Saying that, he produced a shawl. "It was the first thing I could find. I think it's Rita's," he added.

She glanced at it. It looked silver in the moonlight. "She's not going to be happy that you took this."

He had a different take on Rita's reaction. Her first concern was the health and well-being of everyone in her household.

"Don't let that gruff exterior fool you," he told Stacy. "She'd be the first one to tell me to get you to wrap this around your shoulders." He continued holding it out to her.

With a sigh, she took it and threw it over her shoulders. "Okay. I put it on. Happy?" she asked, looking anything but that herself.

His mouth quirked in a grin. "Delirious," he responded.

She thought it best if she changed the subject to something neutral, rather than go on looking up into his eyes, because she'd wind up drowning here. So she turned to look at the land stretching out to infinity beyond the ranch house.

"You know, traveling around with Aunt Kate and going to all those cities that she wanted to see, I forgot how peaceful and quiet it is out here."

He couldn't quite make out if she thought that was a good thing—or a bad one. "Some people would say that translates into *deadly dull*. A lot of people who grow up in Forever can't wait to spread their wings and do exactly what you did—see the world."

She hadn't left because she wanted to see the world; she'd left because she needed to get away from him, away from the pain of being here. But she wasn't about to get into that again. She struggled to focus her thoughts and not get caught up in Cole and the way things had once been.

Going back to what he'd just said, Stacy asked him, "Didn't you ever want to do that?"

He looked at her for a long moment, as if weighing whether or not to answer her. Trying very hard not to get lost in eyes that had always been his undoing. Finally, he asked, "Honestly?"

"Of course."

"No," he told her. "I like it here. I like knowing everyone who lives near and around Forever. Like the feeling of accomplishment when I can help someone—not some anonymous stranger, but a neighbor, someone I *know.* And everyone's a neighbor around here." He smiled to himself, thinking of how that had to sound to her after her extended European vacation. "I guess that someone as sophisticated as you probably finds that kind of simplistic."

"No," Stacy answered. "Since we're being honest—" She took a breath, then said, "I find that kind of heartwarming."

"No you don't."

His response made her temper flare. Before she could tamp it down, she heard herself saying, "Don't tell me what I think or don't think. You don't know me as well as you think you do."

That brought up old wounds. "I found that out eight months ago."

The moment was ruined. She wasn't about to rehash their past. There was no point to that and it wouldn't change anything that happened.

"I think you're right," she said, her voice taking a distant, formal tone. "It is cold out here. I should be getting back inside." She grasped at the first excuse she could think of. "It's probably time to feed or change one of the twins."

"Connor said he'd watch them."

"That doesn't make it any warmer out here," she told him, turning on her heel to go inside.

"Maybe not," Cole agreed.

But instead of following her inside, Cole moved and blocked her path. When she looked at him in confusion, he made no verbal response, tendered no excuse. Instead, he took hold of her shoulders and did what she'd been aching for him to do from the first moment she'd seen him in Miss Joan's diner.

He kissed her.

And she knew instantly that she wasn't over him.

Damn it, Stacy thought as she laced her arms around his neck, she really wasn't over him.

After all the hurt feelings, all the promises she'd made to herself about never opening up her heart to Cole again, she wasn't over him. Because if she were over him, she'd be pushing Cole away from her as hard as she could. And just as he would have looked at her, startled by her display of combined anger and strength, she would have told him what he could do with himself and those lips of his.

Those lethal, lethal lips.

But instead, Stacy found herself melting against him, kissing Cole back as hard as he was kissing her. Holding on to him when she should have been doubling up her fists and punching him, instead.

But she couldn't.

And didn't.

Because for the first time in more than eight very long months, she felt alive again. Eight months filled with going to museums and cafés, of seeing sights that others only read about, of touring places where history had once been made. She'd done all this and *none* of it made her pulse rush and her head spin the way both were doing right at this moment.

Where was her strength? Her self-respect?

Where the hell was *she*? Stacy silently demanded of herself.

She was absolutely lost in a kiss that not only took her breath away, but blotted out her mind, whisking her off to a place that only Cole could create for her.

This wasn't right. And yet she couldn't make herself pull free—and a part of her was praying that what was happening right now would never end.

Chapter Twelve

Cole could feel his heart slamming against his chest, making it hard for him to breathe. His pulse was racing, just the way it used to whenever he and Stacy were together like this.

Right at this moment, all he really wanted to do was pick her up in his arms and take her to his bed so they could make love. But even in his growing ardor, he knew that wasn't really possible. He'd left Connor upstairs with the twins in their room. His brother could come out at any moment.

And heaven only knew where Rita was. The woman had an uncanny knack of popping up at the most inopportune times, not to mention that in all likelihood Connor would hear them once they were upstairs in his room.

Much as he hated to admit it, this couldn't go any further.

Not tonight.

And he knew that if he continued kissing Stacy like this, despite his common sense, it definitely would go further. He was only human and had just so much self-control before he cracked. Every single fiber of his being wanted to make love with her.

What makes you think she wants to make love with you? the voice in his head mocked.

It was the voice of logic, but right now logic had very little to do with the way he was feeling.

Still, at least for now, he had to back off. Better to wait than to be shot down.

So, with the greatest reluctance, Cole ended the kiss and drew back his head. He had a feeling that an apology was due her, but it wouldn't come. All he could say was, "Lord, but I've missed you."

Stacy desperately tried to steel herself. A little more than eight months ago, Cole had pushed her away. Not physically but verbally. Even so, she was the one who had disappeared, not Cole.

And she'd left with just reason, but still, the act of actually leaving Forever—and him—had been hers. So, maybe, on some level, she should be explaining why—or at least telling him she was sorry.

But all that came out of her mouth now was, "I guess maybe I missed you, too."

Not exactly the greatest words of love to go down in the annals of history, Cole thought, but he knew that for someone like Stacy, who had a great deal of pride and trouble accepting fault, this was nothing if not a huge step forward.

Bending slightly toward her, Cole inclined his head and leaned his forehead against hers.

"I guess maybe we should go in before Rita comes out to find out what happened to us."

Stacy didn't really want to go inside. She wanted to stay out here, with him. But she'd be far safer going into the house.

Safer, not from Cole, but from herself.

Because she could feel herself succumbing to him, just the way she had the first time. But as glorious as that felt then, there would be consequences in the aftermath. And this time, she felt she had obligations. She couldn't just run off. Not until the twins' mother turned up.

"What if she doesn't turn up?" Stacy asked suddenly as they walked into the house.

"Rita?" he asked, slightly confused. Was she talking about the housekeeper coming out to look for them?

"No." Stacy's tone was impatient. "The twins' mother," she clarified. "What if the twins' mother doesn't turn up and the sheriff can't find her? What then?"

"It's been less than a month."

"What if she doesn't turn up?" Stacy repeated more insistently. "What are you going to do with the twins?"

Cole paused. He knew how Stacy felt about going to social services so soon, and now that he'd had time to think about it himself, he had to admit that he agreed with her on that score. That didn't exactly leave many options open to him.

Still, he shrugged away Stacy's concern. "I'll think of something. Something'll come up." Cole knew that sounded vague and nebulous, but it was the best he could do for now.

"And if it doesn't?" Stacy pressed.

"It will," Cole countered. Right now, he couldn't promise any more than that.

Coming up to them, her hands on her hips, Rita regarded both of them critically. "If you two are going to argue like this, go back outside."

Remembering that Cole had given her the housekeeper's shawl, Stacy quickly removed it from her shoulders and held it out to Rita.

"I think this is yours," she told the woman. "Thank you for letting me use it."

Rita's expression temporarily softened long enough for her to murmur, "Don't mention it."

Time for her to make her retreat, Stacy thought. "Well, I'd better go check on the twins," she said, one hand on the banister as she was about to go upstairs.

Rita's words stopped her in midstep. "They are asleep."

Stacy looked at the housekeeper, curious. "How can you tell?"

"When they are awake and need something, they cry. You can hear them through the floor," Rita told them, pointing toward the ceiling above her. "Do you hear anything through the floor?"

Stacy listened for a moment, then shook her head. "No."

"Then they are asleep," Rita concluded. A warning look came into her eyes. "Don't you go in now and wake them up, you hear me?" she told Stacy. "Not after all of Mr. Connor's hard work," the woman added as Connor came downstairs at the tail end of her words.

"I didn't work that hard," Connor assured the two women.

Rather than accept the man's protest, Rita gave him a withering look. "Do not contradict me."

"Wouldn't dream of it," Connor assured her.

He flashed the housekeeper a smile, the same one that always professed to the woman that they were on the same page and that he would never go against anything that she said.

"Good," Rita declared. "Then we understand each other—as we always do," she added, a slight twinkle coming into her eye. "If none of you require anything, I think I will go to bed. It has been a long day—and there is a book that I would like to finish."

"A book?" Stacy echoed, curious. She couldn't picture the woman immersing herself in anything other than the day-to-day realities of life at the ranch. "What kind of a book?"

"The old-fashioned kind. One with pages in it," Rita replied, her tone signaling that the conversation was going no further.

With that, the housekeeper turned on her heel and went to her quarters, which were at the rear of the house behind the kitchen.

"I didn't know Rita liked to read," Cole commented, turning toward his brother. "Did you?"

"No, but I suspect that there's a lot about Rita that we don't know," Connor told him.

"Aren't you the least bit curious what she reads?" Cole asked.

"Sure," Connor freely admitted, "but Rita deserves to have her privacy. She'll tell us if she wants us to know something," he added. And then he turned toward Stacy. "The twins are both sleeping at the same time for a change. I suggest that maybe you should turn in, too, and take advantage of that rare situation while you can."

"Maybe I will, at that," Stacy decided.

She was careful to avoid looking in Cole's direction, afraid that he might think she was talking about something other than just going to sleep.

Stacy had to admit that she'd been tempted—sorely tempted—earlier, but once she came back into the house and the full impact of what she'd been thinking of doing hit her, she knew that she couldn't give in to Cole—or herself, for that matter.

As much as he stirred her blood, there was no reason to think that this wouldn't all blow up on her again. A little more than eight months wasn't exactly a huge amount of time. There was no reason to think that Cole had actually changed his thinking when it came to what might be their future together.

He'd told her that he needed his space then. He probably still did. The fact that they were both under the same roof now only gave him the opportunity to give that classic old saying a try: having his cake and eating it, too.

Well, she wasn't a piece of cake and she wasn't about to let him sample anything more than he just had out on the front porch. If she did, she was convinced that she'd be the one to regret it.

Saying good-night to Connor and then, in a more reserved voice, to Cole, Stacy made her way upstairs to her room.

Closing the door, she locked it for good measure— just in case Cole was tempted to come in while she was sleeping.

Or is that wishful thinking on your part? a little voice in her head asked, taunting her.

She was too tired for this.

Damn that man, anyway. Cole's kiss had stirred up things he had no business stirring up. And the sooner she got to sleep, Stacy told herself, putting on her night-gown, the better off she'd be.

Except that she couldn't get to sleep.

Not for a long, long time.

Instead, Stacy tossed and turned, fervently hoping that somewhere along the line, sleep would somehow sneak up on her.

But the only thing that did sneak up on her were memories that she'd thought she'd successfully managed to bury. Obviously, she was wrong. Those memories weren't buried. They were very, very fresh.

This was all Cole's fault. If he hadn't kissed her, she'd be well on her way to getting over him.

Who are you kidding? Your pulse starts to rise any time he gets close to you. If you really wanted to get over him, you wouldn't be here, *you'd be at the hotel, clerking for Rebecca.*

With a deep, weary sigh, Stacy attempted to punch her pillow into a more comfortable, more accommodating shape. She failed.

IT TOOK HER a long time to finally drift off. Just before she fell asleep, she promised herself that she was never letting Cole get close enough to kiss her again.

Never!

She woke up feeling more tired than when she'd gone to bed.

It took her a few moments to realize that one reason could be that she'd been dreaming about Cole. It seemed like even her subconscious mind was ganging up against her.

So then she tried to remember what she'd dreamed about. But the more she tried, the more elusive and out of reach her dreams became. All she could recall was that the dreams were about Cole and that when she'd finally woken up, she was smiling from ear to ear.

Sitting up in bed, Stacy dragged her hand through her hair, struggling to come to and pull herself together.

It was after she'd finished washing her face and while she was still brushing her teeth that she noticed almost seven hours had passed by since Connor had said he'd put the twins to bed.

They'd slept through the night!

That seemed almost impossible, given their age. Stacy remembered hearing that, on the average, babies usually slept through the night only by the time they reached about four months—if their parents were lucky.

"I guess the twins are really exceptional," she said aloud, feeling a tinge of pride for a second.

However, that was followed, for some reason, by a sense of urgency. It swept over her, starting in the pit of her stomach and quickly progressing on to the rest of her.

Something was wrong.

She could feel it.

Stacy quickly threw on her clothes, all the while telling herself that she was overreacting and letting her imagination run away with her. After all, she had no real experience when it came to dealing with babies and she really had no reason to suspect that something might be wrong.

She just did.

Even so, Stacy forced herself to calm down before she left her bedroom. The last thing she wanted was to have Connor or Cole thinking she was some crazy person, given to flights of fantasy and anticipating the very worst for no reason.

After putting on her shoes, she took a deep breath and left her bedroom, then immediately went into the twins' room.

They were both in their crib. Drawing closer, she saw their little chests were subtly moving up and down.

See, they're breathing. You're just being paranoid.

Calm now, Stacy turned away and was about to tiptoe out again.

She had no idea what made her turn back again, or what made her lean over the crib railing and kiss first Katie's forehead and then Mikey's, but she did.

The twins were both burning up.

Chapter Thirteen

Stacy's heart instantly felt as if it had constricted and was now lodged in her throat. Rushing out of the twins' room, she knocked urgently on Cole's door.

"Cole, wake up!" she cried through the door. "They're sick, the twins are really sick!"

As if in unison, the door she was knocking on as well as the one next to it, Connor's door, flew open. The oldest McCullough was wide awake, wearing a pair of old jeans and shrugging into his shirt.

"Sick how?" he asked.

"What's wrong with them?" Cole asked, his voice blending with his brother's. "Give me details." Shirtless, he was the first one into the twins' room.

"They're burning up," Stacy told them. She was doing her best to stay calm, but it wasn't working. All sorts of soul-draining scenarios were flooding her head.

"Have you taken their temperature?" Connor asked.

She looked at him blankly for a second before she felt her brain kicking in. "Do you have a baby thermometer?"

Connor shook his head as he followed her into the

twins' room. Cole, already there, was passing his hand over first one small forehead, then the other. He was frowning.

"If we had one," Connor told her, "either Devon or Cassidy took it with them when they left. There wasn't any need to have a baby thermometer—until now."

"All you have to do is touch them to know that they're running a fever," Stacy told Connor. "Their foreheads and little bodies are really hot."

"She's right," Cole told his brother. "They are."

Wanting to see for himself, Connor went the old-fashioned route. He pressed his lips against each of the twins' foreheads the way he remembered his mother doing whenever Cody or Cole were sick.

Straightening up again, he nodded grimly. "You're right," he told Stacy. "They are hot."

"I hate being right," she retorted. "Shouldn't we be trying to lower their temperatures by immersing them in a tub of cold water or something?" For some reason, she recalled reading an article once describing lowering a baby's temperature using that method.

Cole thought he had a better idea. "Why don't we get them to the clinic?" he said, looking from Stacy to Connor. "They probably need medicine and one of the doctors at the clinic would know the best one to prescribe."

Stacy glanced at the watch that was hardly ever off her wrist. "Isn't it too early for the clinic to be open yet?"

"I'll call Dr. Dan at his house," Connor told Stacy,

adding as he walked out of the room, "You two get them ready to drive into town."

Stacy's hands were shaking as she tried to slip a pull-over shirt and a pair of pants over Katie's sleepwear. She didn't want to risk the baby getting chilled when she was being taken out to the truck.

Cole noticed the way her hands shook. "They're going to be all right," he assured her, his voice low, comforting. "Babies run fevers all the time. It's just the first time it happens that's the scariest."

He sounded so calm, Stacy thought. How did he do it? "You're not worried?" she asked Cole, slipping a hat on the baby.

Katie was fussing, resisting being dressed. It was obvious that she was miserable and cranky. Lying next to her, Mikey was whimpering.

"I didn't say that," Cole answered. "I am," he admitted. "I just know that this is not unusual."

"It is to me," Stacy told him, fervently wishing that she was the one with the fever, not either one of the twins.

Connor came back into the bedroom. "Okay, I called Dr. Dan. He said he'd meet us at the clinic."

"You've got work to do here," Cole reminded his older brother. "No sense in all three of us going to the clinic with the twins."

"But—" Connor began to protest.

"That's okay, I've got this," Cole assured him. "Stacy can sit in the back, holding one of the twins, the other can make the trip in the basket I found them in. They can't both fit in there anymore, but if I put one of them in it, he'll still fit. I'll strap the basket in with a seat belt." Cole could see what his brother was thinking.

"Way ahead of you, Connor," he said. "The second we get back from the clinic and bring the twins home, I'm heading back into town to buy a couple of car seats at the emporium so that we can transport the babies safely."

Connor still appeared a little dubious. "Sure you don't want me to drive?"

"I've got this," Cole repeated, taking out the keys to his truck.

"Maybe you should put a shirt on?" Connor tactfully suggested.

Cole glanced down at his chest. "Oh. Right. One second," he told them, hurrying back into his bedroom.

"And boots," Connor called after him.

"Right!"

Less than a minute later, Cole was back in the twins' bedroom, pulling on a work shirt. Closing a few buttons, he tucked his shirt into his jeans and looked at Stacy. "You ready?"

She barely nodded. "Let's go," she urged, holding Katie against her. She could feel the heat from the baby's little body permeating her own skin. If anything, it felt as if Katie's temperature had gone up.

They all hurried outside to Cole's truck. Stacy handed Katie off to Connor so she could get into the back seat.

He gave the twin back to her, then helped secure the

seat belt around both of them. Meanwhile, Cole had placed Mikey in the wicker basket, then pulled the seat belt tightly around it before pushing the metal tongue into the slot.

Without a word, Cole rounded the rear of the truck to get to the driver's side.

"Last offer," Connor said as Cole climbed in behind the steering wheel.

Cole flashed him a heartfelt smile. He was grateful for the offer, but at the same time, he knew how the work on the ranch was beginning to pile up. He'd cut back on his time at the Healing Ranch in order to juggle helping out with the twins with working on the family ranch alongside of Connor.

"Thanks, but we'll be okay," Cole told him. "All of us. Tell Rita I'm going to be hungry when we get back so she should set a big breakfast aside for me and one for Stacy."

"Yeah, I'll be sure to tell her," Connor told him. "Call me when you know anything." He closed both doors, but the windows were each cracked open so they could hear him.

"In Cole's case, that might not be for a long time," Stacy quipped. It was her way of trying to stave off another attack of nerves.

"Call anyway," Connor said with a smile.

He stepped back as his brother started the truck.

Within a few moments they had pulled away from the main house and were on the road that led straight into Forever.

There was only the sound of the twins, fussing and whimpering for several miles. Cole could almost *feel* Stacy's tension as it continued to grow in the truck.

This couldn't be good for her.

"At least we don't have to worry about running into traffic here," Cole said in an attempt to distract Stacy and draw her into a conversation.

"Just the occasional stray mountain lion," Stacy commented. She didn't even bother looking up. Her attention was entirely focused on the two babies in the back seat.

"It's a big truck," Cole answered. "I can outrun a mountain lion if it comes to that." He glanced up into the rearview mirror to catch a glimpse of her face, "How are you holding up?"

"I'm not the one running a high fever."

"No," he replied, "you're the one who looks as pale as a ghost."

She didn't want any attention focused on her. She was too worried about the twins. "I didn't get a chance to put my makeup on."

This time when he looked up into the rearview mirror, his eyes met hers for a split second. "You don't wear any makeup."

She felt herself growing defensive. "Done right, it's not supposed to look like there's any makeup on at all."

"Then what's the point?"

"A question for the ages," she answered. And definitely one she didn't think merited discussion. "Can this thing go any faster?" she asked.

"Yes," he answered patiently. "But I don't want to shake the twins up."

She just wanted to get them to the doctor as quickly as possible. "Their fevers are practically sky high. I don't think they'll notice."

"Okay, faster it is," he told her, giving in and throwing the truck into fifth gear.

The truck responded instantly.

THEY MADE IT to Forever in record time and drove right past Miss Joan's diner and several other establishments, coming to a screeching halt right in front of the clinic.

Dan was standing there, obviously waiting for them. He moved toward the truck the moment he saw them approaching.

"Bring them inside to the first exam room," he told them, waving the two adults into the clinic.

By now the twins were both crying, very vocal in registering their mutual distress.

Cole carried Mikey while Stacy brought in Katie.

Holding the baby to herself, she was murmuring to the little girl, saying anything and everything that came into her head in an effort to soothe the infant a little— and maybe herself in the process.

Because it was too early for either of the nurses to have come in yet, Dan had Stacy provide the extra set of hands he needed during each exam. When he finished with Katie, he handed the infant over to Cole and had Stacy help him with Mikey.

The entire time he conducted his examination, Stacy

never took her eyes off Dan. She was watching the doctor's every move, gauging his every expression so that she could determine whether or not Dr. Davenport was telling her the truth about the babies' condition, or if he was just handing her a bunch of platitudes to keep her from overreacting.

She'd liked the doctor ever since he first came to Forever, but this was different. This involved two tiny human beings who had managed, without any effort at all, to wrap her heart around their tiny little fingers. She cared deeply about their welfare.

She didn't realize she was holding her breath until Cole leaned over and whispered, "Breathe," into her ear.

She shivered, shrugged off his words and moved a few inches away from him. Any farther and her view of the twins would have been obstructed.

She made an elaborate display of drawing in a big breath.

"Better," Cole mouthed.

She pretended she hadn't seen him do it.

Finally finished with his exam, Dan prepared two syringes, each filled with acetaminophen. He proceeded to inject a dose into the upper portion of first Katie's and then Mikey's chubby little upper thigh.

Stacy winced each time the needle went in. The babies didn't seem to even feel it. There was no change in their whimpering.

"Why did you just give them shots?" she asked.

"That was to lower their temperatures. A shot works faster than oral medication." The doctor carefully threw the syringes he'd used into a self-sealing hazardous waste container. "Their temperatures should be going down by the time you get them back to your ranch," Dan estimated.

That was best-case scenario. She wanted to be prepared for what happened if it wasn't.

"And if not?" Stacy challenged. "What if their temperatures remain high?"

Dan glanced in her direction for half a second, saying, "You give it a little longer."

She needed more than something so vague to go on. "How much longer?" Stacy asked, taking in a jagged breath.

Dan paused, as if to weigh a few factors, then answered, "An hour, at most. If their fevers still don't go down—which would be highly unusual—bring them back."

"And then what?" she asked.

"I'll keep them here for observation," Dan answered her calmly. He put a comforting hand on her shoulder. "One way or another, we're going to lick this thing, so don't worry."

She let out a shaky breath. "I hope you're right, Doctor."

"So do I, Stacy. So do I," he told her with a warm smile. "Wait here," he said, stepping out of the exam room. "I'll be right back."

"What do you think he's doing?" Stacy asked, gazing after the doctor. Picking up Katie, she cradled the baby against her and began rocking her.

"Possibly getting tranquilizers for you," Cole told her, picking up the other twin.

She turned to look at him. "Me?"

He pinned her with a look. "You're about to go off like a Roman candle. I think he's worried about you."

"*He's* worried about me?" she questioned, knowing that Cole was actually referring to himself.

"Maybe we're all worried about you. But you're not going to do these babies—or yourself—any good if you don't get a grip on yourself, Stacy."

She'd just about had it with his advice. "You told me that I wasn't going to be of any use to them if I didn't get some sleep. So I got some sleep and look what happened," she cried, looking down at Katie. "They're sick."

"Stace, your sleeping had nothing to do with them getting sick," Cole insisted.

"But if I wasn't asleep, I would have realized they were coming down with fevers and I could have called the doctor *before* it got to be this bad."

"And if you had wings and a propeller, you could be a plane."

She stared at him. "That doesn't make any sense."

"And neither are you," Cole told her. He could see that she didn't understand. "Take a deep breath. Calm down," he ordered. "The doc's the best there is. You've got to have a little faith, Stacy."

Stacy felt tears forming in her eyes. She tried to blink them back, but they only slipped out.

"They're so little. And so helpless," she told him, her voice cracking.

Cole put his arm around her. "And they're going to grow up nice and healthy and bigger than you are," he told her. "Trust me."

Stacy let out a very shaky breath. "It's not up to you."

"No," Cole agreed. "But the faith part comes in when you have it about the one who it *is* up to."

She found herself wishing she could be like Cole: easygoing and trusting. "It's not as easy for me as it is for you," she told him.

He smiled at Stacy. "It's not easy for me."

Dan walked in just then with a box of small packets in his hands. "I want you to dissolve one of these in each of their bottles twice a day until the packets are all gone. That should take care of any remaining fever as well as the infection they seemed to have gotten. It's not as uncommon as you think," he assured Stacy and Cole. "Call me anytime if you have any questions or concerns, but if all goes well, these two are going to be back to their normal, healthy, noisy little selves within twenty-four hours," Dan promised.

"That fast?" Stacy questioned uncertainly.

Dan nodded. "Kids can have a high fever in the morning, be fine in the afternoon and suffer a slight relapse in the evening only to be a hundred percent well the next morning. They're resilient that way. The bad news is that this sort of thing goes on until they're about seven, so brace yourselves, you're in for a bumpy ride," he told them with a laugh. "Between you and me, as a proud father of three, I wouldn't have it any other way."

She felt just the slightest bit better. "I can't thank you enough," Stacy told the doctor.

"You already have. Now, I've got to excuse myself," he told them, crossing the threshold. "I've got a clinic to open up."

Turning away from them, he went to do just that.

Chapter Fourteen

The babies' fevers broke before noon, first Mikey's, then Katie's. By one o'clock, both babies' foreheads were cool.

Even so, Stacy refused to let either one of the twins out of her sight. She held them, rocked them and sang to them, separately and together.

Clucking her tongue at Stacy, Rita brought her lunch to the twins' bedroom. When she came to clear away the tray an hour later, the housekeeper obviously saw that nothing had been touched.

Rather than picking it up, Rita just looked down at the tray, frowning.

"You don't like my cooking?" she questioned. However, instead of taking offense, the way Stacy expected her to, the woman actually made her an offer. "I can bring you something else."

Stacy gave the older woman a contrite smile. "I'm really not hungry right now, Rita. Why don't you just leave that?" she suggested. Sitting in the rocking chair, she was rocking Mikey to sleep. Katie had already drifted off and was in the crib, asleep. "I'll eat it later."

Rita's frown deepened just a tad. "Later it won't be warm."

"I'm sure it's good cold, too," Stacy told the housekeeper. "Everything you make is delicious."

Rita leveled a look at her, as if to tell her that flattery wasn't going to get her off the hook. "Mr. Cole and Mr. Connor won't be happy when they come back and find out that you are not eating."

It had been hard enough convincing Cole that he could leave and help Connor with the horses when they got back to the house with the twins this morning. She didn't need him clucking over her the way Rita was doing.

Stacy offered the woman her widest, albeit weariest smile. "Then we won't tell him, will we?"

Rita passed her hand over Mikey's forehead, no doubt to reassure herself that the baby's fever was gone.

"Maybe *you* won't," Rita began.

Stacy went all out in her appeal. "Rita, please. I just had the scare of my life with these two little ones. They're getting better, but my appetite's going to need some time to recover. The last thing I want—or need— is a lecture from Cole."

Rita pressed her lips together, a sure sign that she was suppressing some well-chosen words.

Sighing dramatically, Rita said, "It is against my better judgment, but have it your way." She paused, lingering over the crib and the other twin. She touched Katie's forehead so lightly the baby didn't wake up. "Thank heavens their fevers are gone." Still looking down at Katie, she glanced over toward the other infant in Stacy's arms. "They are getting bigger. Soon they are going to need to be in separate cribs."

Stacy thought of the money her aunt had left her. There wasn't enough for a lavish lifestyle, but that sort of thing had never interested her. She just needed enough to get by until she eventually found work. But for now, since she was still staying here, she could afford to buy a second crib.

"That won't be a problem," Stacy told the housekeeper.

Rita said something under her breath in Spanish. Stacy couldn't tell from the woman's tone if she was saying something antagonistic, merely critical or just neutral. For now, Stacy thought it was more prudent to just let it go. She felt too tired and dull to engage in any sort of a lengthy verbal exchange.

After Rita left, Stacy rose from the rocking chair, and moving very slowly, she laid the sleeping infant in the crib near his twin. She held her breath, waiting, but Mikey continued sleeping, as did Katie.

Stacy returned to her rocking chair. Wanting to be there the minute one or both of the twins woke up, she sat, waiting.

It wasn't too long before Stacy found herself dozing off. She knew that she could just go to her own room right next door, but for now proximity meant everything to her. She needed to reassure herself that the twins were all right the minute she opened her eyes.

A SUDDEN, UNEXPECTED thunderstorm delayed Cole and Connor's return to the house. Not because any road was washed out—there wasn't enough rain for that—but because the thunder wound up spooking a couple of the horses. They broke out of the corral and took off for open country.

Cole and Connor were forced to go after the two stallions, wanting to find them before it got dark and the horses ran the risk of falling prey to one or more of the hungry wolves that had been sighted in the area.

It wasn't easy, but they kept at it until they managed to find both horses.

It was well after seven by the time they brought the horses back to the stable and finally walked into the house.

As if they had phoned ahead to tell her they were returning, Rita was right there when they opened the front door.

"I have seen drowned rats that have looked better," Rita told them emotionlessly, greeting the two men at the door with towels.

"You're a saint, Rita," Connor said, taking one of the towels from her and drying off his face and hair.

"Albeit a sharp-tongued one," Cole couldn't help commenting, taking the other towel and vigorously rubbing it over his head. He felt as if he was wet clear down to the bone. "What about the twins?" he asked. He hadn't seen the babies in the last eight hours and he had found himself worrying about them. "How are they doing?"

"Much better. Their appetites are back and they finished their bottles. Twice," Rita happily reported. "Which is more than I can say for Miss Stacy."

Cole stopped toweling his hair and looked at the woman. "What do you mean?" he asked.

"I mean that she has not been out of their room except to get their bottles," Rita answered, disapproval dripping from each word.

Connor placed the towel down on the coffee table. "Has she eaten?" he asked Rita.

"No. I have brought her two trays, one with her lunch, one with her dinner when you did not return at the usual time." She paused for effect, then said, "I left the second tray next to the first one. I am willing to bet that they are both still exactly where I put them, untouched."

That was all he needed. Cole hurried over to the stairs.

"You need to eat, too," Rita called after him. "And to get out of those wet clothes."

"Later," he tossed over his shoulder, taking the stairs two at a time to the second floor.

Stacy stifled a startled squeal when the door to the twins' room flew open and Cole walked in, leaving drops of rainwater on the floor to mark his passage.

"You get caught in the rain?"

He saw the trays butted up against each other. As Rita had predicted, there was nothing touched on either one of them. Didn't Stacy realize that she needed to keep up her strength? Sometimes, she could really exasperate him—or was that just frustration because he wanted her so much? Wanted what he knew he couldn't have. She'd made that clear by leaving Forever with her aunt.

"No," he answered Stacy sarcastically. "I swam back home."

Stacy didn't even react to his sarcasm. She blinked, trying to focus and wishing he wouldn't look at her like that, making her feel vulnerable. Taking a breath, she asked Cole, "What time is it, anyway?"

"Late," he answered. Taking a breath and telling himself that upbraiding her for not taking care of herself would just have the opposite effect on her—she had always been as contrary as hell—he tried talking to her as if they were nothing more than friends. "The thunder spooked a couple of the horses. It took us this long to find them."

She nodded, as if this was an everyday occurrence. "You should change," she told him, looking down at the puddle forming at his feet. "And eat."

He found her suggestion ironic. "I could say the same thing to you."

"Why?" Too tired to get out of the rocking chair, Stacy remained sitting and gazed up at Cole. "I haven't been out in the rain."

"According to Rita, you've hardly been out of the room. And you haven't eaten," he said, gesturing toward the two trays the housekeeper had prepared and left on top of the bureau.

"The twins' fever is gone, just like Dr. Dan told us it would be."

As far as Cole was concerned, it only reinforced the point he was trying to get across to her. "Then why haven't you eaten?"

Stacy lifted her shoulders in a half shrug. "I'm not really hungry. I could stand to lose a few pounds," she interjected, hoping he'd accept that not eating was a choice on her part.

His eyes washed over her. "Only if you want to fill in as some farmer's scarecrow," he replied. "If you lose a few pounds, Stacy, you're going to be nothing but skin and bones."

Stacy laughed drily. "Words every woman wants to hear."

"You want words every woman wants to hear?" His hands on either side of the rocking chair's arms, he leaned in and with his face less than five inches from hers, he told her, "Go to bed."

Stacy raised her chin defensively. "You're not in charge of me."

"I am if you collapse in my house," Cole countered. Taking her by the wrist, he was about to raise her out of the chair and take her over to the neglected trays of food.

Annoyed, Stacey yanked her wrist free. Didn't he think she could take care of herself? That she knew if she needed to eat or not?

"I'm fine," she snapped at him. "Now go take care of yourself. Eat. And for heaven's sake, change your clothes." She wrinkled her nose. "You smell of rain and sweat."

He sighed, knowing it would do no good to argue with Stacy when she was like this. Turning on his heel, he walked out.

She was right, he needed to get out of his wet clothes. More than that, he needed to cool off. She'd managed, in the space of a few minutes, to press all his buttons, and right now he didn't trust himself not to say things to her that he couldn't take back once he calmed down.

"How is she?" Connor asked when Cole finally came downstairs again, this time in dry clothes.

"Peppery," Cole answered, sitting down at the dining room table.

"Well, I think you've come to expect that," Connor commented. He had already helped himself to the pot roast as well as an assortment of vegetables that Rita had made for dinner. "Still, I always liked Stacy. If you ask my opinion—"

Cole took a serving of pot roast. He was choosier with the vegetables, taking only the potatoes and carrots. "I'm going to get it if I ask for it or not, aren't I?" he asked stoically.

Connor went on as if his brother hadn't said anything. "She's the nicest girl out of all the ones you ever went out with. I actually thought the two of you were getting close to a commitment." He paused before asking, "What happened?"

Cole avoided his brother's eyes. "She took off," he

said matter-of-factly, stating something that they were both aware of.

"And you didn't have anything to do with that?" Connor asked his brother.

Cole put his fork down and sighed as he looked at his brother. "Why all the questions? You really need a life, Connor," he concluded.

"I have a life." Connor finished the piece of roast beef he was eating. "The ranch and my family are my life, and right now, one of my family is in danger of having the best thing that ever happened to him slip through his fingers."

Cole looked at him, confused. "Just how did we go from my saying she's peppery to this?"

"When you're my age, you get pretty good at filling in the blanks," Connor answered.

Ignoring his dinner, Cole just stared at his brother. "What do you mean, *your age*? You're only two years older than I am," he pointed out.

"And a hell of a lot smarter, apparently," Connor said. "All I'm saying is that Stacy left once. She's back now so you've got another chance. Make sure you don't wind up blowing it."

He wanted to tell Connor that he was wrong, that his big brother was sticking his nose into something that didn't concern him. But in both cases, Cole couldn't say that. Because having Stacy back *did* feel like a second chance and, just as importantly, because they were McCulloughs and family business *was* their business—

even if it drove him crazy to be the recipient of all this so-called wise advice from Connor.

"I won't blow it," Cole finally said. "As long as you promise to back off a little." He finished his vegetables first. He'd always liked ending his meal with meat. "You know I'm not at my best with you looking over my shoulder, watching my every move."

"Well, somebody's got to keep you from going over the cliff—but I'll back off," Connor said to placate Cole for the time being. "Are the twins doing okay?"

Relieved to change the subject, Cole nodded. "The worst of it seems to be over. You know—" he reached for the apple pie and cut himself a slice now that he'd finished with dinner "—I don't know how Mom and Dad did it, Mom with the three of us and Dad with all four." Suddenly, all the sacrifices that his older brother had made for them came to mind. "For that matter, I really don't know how you did it."

Connor smiled. "Well, for one thing, I didn't have much of a choice."

That was a crock and Connor knew it, Cole thought. "Yes, you did. You could have just gone off to college like you were planning to before Dad died."

Finished, Connor pushed his dinner plate aside. "And what kind of a person would that have made me?" he asked. "Leaving the three of you to be split up and placed with who knows what kind of people? I might be selfish, but I'm not *that* selfish."

Cole looked at his brother as if Connor had taken leave of his senses. "You don't have a selfish bone in your body. You never had. And I guess I never said this to you," he said, feeling a tinge of guilt, "but I really appreciate the sacrifice you made for Cody and Cassidy and me. And I know that they do."

Obviously embarrassed, Connor shrugged off his brother's gratitude. "We were all in this together. No need to thank me."

"Yeah, there is," Cole insisted. "I never really thought much about it until now, but there's a *huge* need to thank you. If you hadn't stepped up the way that you did, there's no telling how any of our lives would have turned out."

"You still would have been you, just as Cody and Cassidy would have still been who they are. Everything would have worked itself out. It usually does."

"Damn it, Connor," Cole said, frustrated, "I'm trying to thank you. Just accept it and stop telling me I don't need to."

"Okay, gratitude accepted," Connor told him. "Now, why don't you go back upstairs and see if you can coax Stacy out with some of Rita's fantastic apple pie?" he suggested, waving his hand at the pie that Rita had baked less than an hour ago. It was going fast. "I just had a piece myself and my mouth is still smiling. If this doesn't get Stacy to eat, nothing will. But get her down here fast before I'm tempted to eat the rest of it."

"I've got a better idea," Cole told him. "I'm going to bodily carry Stacy out of the room and bring her down to the table."

"You're going to strong-arm her?" Connor asked.

"I'd do it carefully if I were you. That little lady is a lot tougher than she looks."

"That's okay," Cole told Connor. "I'll just toss her over my shoulder, fireman style."

Connor didn't bother hiding his amused smile as he helped himself to more pie. "If you say so."

Taking the piece he had cut for Stacy, Cole didn't bother answering as he left the room.

A little extra ammunition never hurt.

Chapter Fifteen

Opening the door to the twins' room slowly so he wouldn't wake them up—if they *were* asleep—Cole held the plate with Rita's pie out in front of him like a peace offering.

"I come bearing apple pie."

When he received no response, Cole pushed the door farther open. And then he saw why Stacy hadn't said anything.

She was slumped in the rocking chair, her head to one side, sound asleep.

Looking at the scene, Cole smiled to himself. "Looks like it all caught with you, didn't it, Stacy? These little guys can really wipe you out if you're not careful."

Once he'd set the pie down on the tray closest to him, he turned his attention back to Stacy. He couldn't just leave her sitting there like that. If nothing else, she was going to wake up with an awfully stiff neck.

Very gently, he slipped one arm under Stacy's legs, the other around her back, and exercising extreme care, he lifted her up off the rocking chair. Watching her face, he half expected her to wake up at any second and demand to be let go.

What he *didn't* expect was to have Stacy curl up against his chest like a pet kitten. The old pull that had once been so much a part of their relationship was back. In spades.

"Good thing for you, you're asleep," he whispered under his breath. Moving carefully, he managed to close the door to the twins' room, then carried Stacy into her bedroom.

He crossed to her bed and gently laid her down. For a second, he just stood there, watching her. And then he sighed. "You tie me up in knots, Stacy. You know that, don't you? I'm not sure how much longer I can stay on my good behavior."

Cole was just pulling the covers over her when, still appearing to be asleep, Stacy caught his arm. The sudden move threw him completely off balance and he fell on her before he could stop himself.

Stacy woke up with a start, pushing him off her and to the floor before she was even fully conscious. Scrambling into a sitting position, she looked down at Cole, glaring at him.

"What the hell do you think you're doing?" she demanded.

Cole laughed drily. He would have thought that the answer would have been self-evident to her. "I'm trying to put you to bed."

"Yes, I can see that."

"No, really," he insisted. "Just you, just bed. You were the one who caught my arm and pulled me down on you. I was just about to tiptoe out again."

Stacy rolled her eyes. "Oh, please, you can't come up with a better story than that?"

"I don't have to," he informed her. "It's the truth." He got up off the floor and dusted off his jeans. She was on her knees on the bed and he towered over her. "You've been here for over three weeks, Stacy. Given our history, don't you think that if I wanted to go to bed with you, I would have been a little more subtle about it than to leap on you while you were asleep?"

Stacy took a deep breath. It made sense, but she still wasn't all that sure. She felt her stomach tightening.

"I don't know. Would you have?" Her heart was pounding in her chest as she asked the question. The next moment, a surge of guilt made her relent. "I'm sorry, that wasn't fair. But you startled me." Still on her knees, she looked around the room blankly. "Where are the twins?"

"In their room. Sleeping peacefully," he added before she could ask. "I just thought that since they were sleeping, maybe you'd like to do the same." He frowned slightly. "I don't want to be rushing off with you to see Dr. Dan in the middle of the night."

She sniffed. "Don't worry. You won't have to. I don't get sick."

"Ah, I had no idea I was in the presence of a superwoman." His tone was slightly mocking. He blew out a breath. "Well, I'd better let you get your rest." He turned to leave, but this time she caught his hand in hers instead of his arm.

Turning back, he looked at Stacy, puzzled, waiting for an explanation.

"Don't go," she requested in a subdued voice. "Stay with me for a while."

That totally disarmed him.

"Okay," Cole responded cautiously.

He sat down on the bed beside her, not knowing what to expect. He tried to focus on the fact that she'd asked him to stay and not on the fact that she looked so desirable or on how much he wanted her. It wasn't easy because all he could think of was that last night they had spent together and how warm, pliant and giving she'd felt in his arms. If he took her into his arms now, would she feel that way again?

Get a grip on yourself, not her, Cole upbraided himself.

"I'm sorry I've been so surly and difficult," she said.

That surprised him. In the face of an apology, he relented and forgave her. "You were worried about the twins. We all were."

"No, I was surly and difficult even before they got sick." She flushed. This was hard for her, but she had to say it for her own peace of mind. "You've been nothing but nice to me since I got here and I've been taking things out on you."

"It's okay," Cole began, not wanting to dig up old wounds. It served no purpose, in his opinion. It could only hurt.

"No, it's *not* okay," Stacy insisted.

He sighed. "Stacy, I'm trying to move forward." He

could see by the look on her face that *forward* wasn't a destination they would be reaching, at least not soon. Feeling as if his back was against the wall, he tried another, albeit blunt, approach. "What do you want from me, Stacy?"

Her eyes held his. "I want you to tell me what happened."

That didn't make any sense to him. "You know what happened. You were there."

"Yes," she acknowledged, "I was. And one minute it was the most wonderful night of my life and the next, you were putting enough distance between us to build another continent."

"You're the one who left."

She squared her shoulders. "Only after you did."

What was she talking about? He'd stayed right here in Forever. She was the one who had taken off. "I didn't leave."

"Yes, you did," Stacy insisted. "You left emotionally."

"You scared me."

Her eyes narrowed. Now he was just making things up. "I'm five foot two. You're over six feet, how could I have possibly scared you?"

"Because of the way I felt about you," he told her. "I thought we were just having a good time, but then suddenly it turned into something so much more. Something really intense." His eyes held hers. "Something, I felt, that was going to change the rest of my life."

"So you disappeared," she concluded.

"I backed off," Cole corrected. "I just needed a little time to get my head together, to deal with what I was feeling. By the time I did," he told her, "you were gone. Gone without a single word." And it had ripped out his heart. "I had no idea where you went or what had happened to you." The mere memory of it frustrated him even now. "Your aunt was gone, too, so I didn't even have anyone to ask."

She shook her head, confused. "I thought you wanted it that way."

"No. I didn't know what I wanted." Cole shifted so that they were only inches apart. "But I do now."

He looked at Stacy, knowing that he was taking a big risk, putting his feelings into words. But if he didn't take a chance, then he would probably lose the one thing that people strove so hard to find. "I want you."

She felt her heart leap up. With effort, she struggled to put it all into perspective. "Don't toy with me, Cole."

"I'm not." He took her hand in his. "I don't expect you to forgive me, or even to believe me. But if you could find it in your heart to—"

Cole never got the chance to finish his sentence. His mother and then his father had drummed it into his head not to talk with his mouth full, and right now, his mouth was completely engaged in something he'd only been dreaming and reminiscing about.

Stacy had sealed her lips to his in a passionate kiss, and all he could think of was that he needed to kiss her back or he'd lose her.

His heart rate accelerated to the point that he doubted

any sort of a medical instrument could accurately register it. It was pounding hard against his chest and if he died now, he didn't care—as long as it was in this moment, a moment he'd been yearning for, praying for, for the last nine months.

Slipping his arms around Stacy, Cole pulled her urgently to him.

The kiss heated and deepened until it completely consumed him. With his pulse racing so fast it made a lightning bolt seem slow, he moved his lips to her throat, to her face, to her eyes, then back to her mouth. The sound of Stacy's heavy breathing echoed in his soul, inciting him.

He wasn't sure just how they wound up lying on her bed, sealed against each other's bodies as passion flared to yet a higher level. Everything seemed blurry to him, happening both quickly and, somehow, also in slow motion.

He began to undress Stacy, eager to feel her, to have her, the way he had that night an eternity ago.

And then he froze.

What the hell are you doing? he silently demanded of himself as he pulled back.

Startled, Stacy looked at him in utter confusion.

"Why did you stop?" she cried. Was he doing it again? Was he pulling away from her? She didn't understand what was going on.

"You're vulnerable and I don't want to take advantage of you," Cole confessed, even though stopping like this was killing him by inches.

Stacy blinked. "I was the one who started kissing you. How does that make *me* vulnerable?"

"Because you're tired—" he began to explain.

"I'm tired," she agreed. "I'm not in a coma. There's a difference," she insisted. "Now, if you're having second thoughts because you don't want me—"

This time, she was the one who didn't get to finish her sentence because this time, struck by the absurdity of what she was about to say, his lips were covering hers. Silencing her.

And this time there was no hesitation on the part of either of them.

It was as if they had suddenly been freed of all impediments, all emotional baggage, and were able to finally act on what they were feeling right at this very moment.

Fire ignited within Stacy.

All the emotions she had struggled so hard to push away and bury, denying what she'd felt for Cole, what she had been feeling for Cole all along, surfaced and burst forward, consuming her and taking her prisoner.

She slid her hands all along Cole's body, touching him, needing to reassure herself that he was real, that he was here. She wasn't just dreaming this the way she had during all those long months touring the European cities that her aunt had always longed to see.

European cities that meant nothing to her because Cole wasn't there to see them with her.

Stacy's breathing was growing faster by the moment, as if she was racing to some invisible finish line. And yet, she was loath to do so, because once she did reach it this exquisite moment in time would be over.

And maybe permanently.

She didn't want it to be over, didn't want him to leave her bed, her room, her life, the way he had the last time. She knew if that happened, she wouldn't be able to survive it again.

This time, there would be no Aunt Kate to rescue her from the deep pit. There would be no hope, no salvation for her, only a vast feeling of emptiness.

COLE COULDN'T GET enough of her.

She was just the way she had been before—but, oh, so much more.

It was as if he had a wildcat on his hands, an untamed spirit that aroused so many desires, so many emotions within him that he couldn't begin to count them. They swarmed around him like the funnel of a twister. He had no choice but to let it take him wherever it was going.

He didn't want this moment to end.

Cole kissed her over and over again, his lips trailing along her body, reacquainting himself with what he had gone over so many times before in his mind. Everything was both familiar and brand new—just the way she was.

And when he could no longer hold himself in check, when he felt that he was about to explode if he held back for even a single moment longer, Cole worked his way up along her body, nipping her tender skin, branding it with his lips and his tongue. Rejoicing in the way she squirmed beneath him, doing her best not to cry out so that she wouldn't be heard and possibly bring the moment to an end.

Cole could tell by the way she moved that he'd created several small climaxes for her, working his way up her body and up to the final moment.

And then he was over her, his eyes holding hers as his body aligned with hers.

Just a little pressure from him and she parted her legs in a silent invitation.

His heart racing, he entered her, sealing his body to hers.

Then it began, the dance that would take them to the one place that they both wanted to reach, the summit that loomed above them, calling to them.

As he moved, Stacy echoed his movements, going faster and faster.

The pace stole away their breaths until it became so fast that they all but set her bed on fire.

She clung to him when the final moment overtook them. The fireworks surrounded them, blotting out everything except for the two of them and the mind-numbing sensation that had been created.

Stacy dug her fingers into his back, as if desperately trying to anchor herself to the moment, to him. Not wanting it to end, not wanting to revert to the world that existed just beyond them, waiting to receive them back into its embrace.

He felt her heart pounding wildly against his chest, felt his own matching it, beat for beat.

Whatever might happen from this moment forward, he would have this. Have it and treasure it.

Embracing Stacy, he held her against him and pressed a single tender kiss to her forehead.

"I love you."

Chapter Sixteen

Stacy froze.

Raising her eyes, she looked at him. Her imagination had to be playing tricks on her, taking a glorious experience and making it into something even more. Something that she knew wasn't true.

He must have felt Stacy suddenly stiffening in his arms.

"I'm sorry," he said quietly.

Well, that was one mystery cleared up. It wasn't her imagination. "So you did say it."

"It just slipped out."

She put her own interpretation to his words. "But you didn't mean it."

He raised his eyes to hers, unable to gauge what she was thinking from her tone of voice. So he had to ask. "Would you want me to?"

Oh, no, he wasn't going to get her to tell him how she felt if he was apologizing for saying the words that she had longed to hear. "I didn't want you to say anything you didn't want to say."

"Oh, the hell with it," he muttered, giving up and pulling her to him.

"What are you doing?" she cried, startled.

Cole grinned wickedly. "If you have to ask, either I didn't do it right the first time, or you are seriously in need of a refresher course. In either case—"

He ended his statement with a kiss—which happily began everything all over again.

SHE WAS GONE from her bed when he woke up.

Dawn was just beginning to paint lighter shades along the darkness on the horizon.

Cole sat up, shaking off the last remnants of sleep. He should have gone to his own room long before now, he upbraided himself. But they'd made love two more times, and after that, he'd been too exhausted to move. He didn't remember falling asleep.

Cole quickly pulled on his jeans and shrugged into his shirt before stepping out into the hallway. He assumed that Stacy was in the twins' room and debated knocking on their door. But if they were, by some chance, asleep again, he didn't want to take a chance on waking them up. So he finally just twisted the doorknob and eased the door opened.

When he walked in, Stacy was already looking in his direction, having anticipated his entrance when she saw the doorknob move.

"Morning," he said, smiling broadly at her.

"It certainly is," Stacy agreed. When she'd slipped

out of bed, he'd been sound asleep. "Did I wear you out?" There was a note of pleasure in her voice.

"In the best possible way," he admitted.

For now, Cole felt it was for the best not to bring up last night. She still hadn't really let him know, one way or another, how she felt about his having said the three most important words one human being could say to another. He didn't know if he had frightened her, or if his loving her was just something she had to get used to.

In any event, she hadn't given him any idea how she felt and certainly hadn't indicated that she felt that way about him, too. If she didn't love him, it wasn't something that he wanted to face right now.

He nodded at the twins, both of whom were awake and kicking their little legs. "How are they?"

"Hungry," she answered. "I changed them and was just about to go downstairs to get their bottles."

"You stay here," he told her. "I'll go get the bottles." He left the room before she could argue the point.

Connor was seated at the table, enjoying his first cup of inky black coffee of the day. Seeing Cole walk into the kitchen, he commented, "Well, you certainly look happy."

"Why shouldn't I be?" Cole asked. "The twins are better, we found the runaway horses, the rain is gone and it's the beginning of a brand-new, beautiful day."

Connor smiled to himself as he took another long sip of his coffee. "Uh-huh."

"I'm going to ignore that," Cole told his brother, taking two bottles filled with formula out of the refrigerator. He warmed them individually.

"Ignore what?" Connor asked innocently. "I'm agreeing with you."

"I know that *uh-huh*. That's the sound you make when you're humoring me."

Connor finished off his coffee. "You're letting your imagination get the better of you." He cocked his head, studying his brother. "Or is that just a guilty conscience?"

Cole's eyes darted toward his brother. Did he know? Had Connor somehow guessed that he had spent the night with Stacy?

Since Connor wasn't saying anything specific, Cole decided to go with denial. "I don't have anything to be guilty about."

"Good to hear. Glad we're on the same page," Connor said, clapping his brother on the shoulder as he put his empty coffee cup in the sink. "It should be a pretty light workday today. You can check in at the Healing Ranch to see if they need you, or—" a whimsical smile playing along his lips "—you can stay here to spell Stacy and take over taking care of the twins. Sounded like she wore herself out yesterday."

Cole avoided making eye contact with his brother. "I think she got some sleep when the twins fell asleep," he said evasively.

The bottles were warm enough and he picked them up to take to Stacy.

"Did she, now?" Connor asked, turning to walk out the front door.

Was he that transparent? Cole wondered. Could Connor guess at and predict his every move even before he made it, at least, when it came to Stacy? Or was Connor just reading things into everything he said, again, because of Stacy?

Cole decided that was a riddle for another time. He had things to do.

Walking back into the twins' bedroom, Cole announced, "Breakfast is served. Why don't you go downstairs and get yourself some while I take care of these guys?"

"My breakfast will keep," she told him. "I want to make sure these little people stay on some sort of a regular schedule, and right now, it's time to feed them."

Cole handed her one of the bottles and held on to the other one himself. "Might as well help you out," he told Stacy.

She tried to take the second bottle from him, but he continued to hold it. Stacy gave up. Nevertheless, she asked, "Don't you have something to do?"

Cole feigned being hurt. "Are you trying to get rid of me?"

She shrugged as she picked up one of the twins and sat down in the rocking chair.

"I just don't want to take you away from what you normally do."

"Stop being so noble," he chided. "You're confusing me."

"Meaning I'm not normally noble?" Stacy asked, a slight edge in her voice.

Cole grinned the moment he heard her tone. "There's that fire I know so well," he told her with a laugh.

Stacy sighed and shook her head. In her arms, Mike greedily went at the bottle she held to his lips. "You're crazy, you know that?"

"Highly possible," Cole agreed. He turned toward the remaining twin in the crib. "Okay, Mikey, time for one of your many feedings," he said, picking the baby up in his arms.

Amused, Stacy corrected him. "That's Katie you just picked up."

He was certain he could tell them apart. "No, it's not."

Stacy merely smiled. "I just changed them before you came in. That's Katie. Trust me."

Well, he couldn't very well argue with anatomy. "Okay, Katie," he began again amicably, "time for one of your many feedings."

Stacy laughed softly, shaking her head. She liked the way that Cole rolled with the punches. He was a lot more adaptable than she was, she'd give him that.

Sitting down on the edge of the nightstand to feed Katie, Cole glanced in Stacy's direction. "Something funny?" he asked.

"No, not really." She didn't really want to tell him she was giving him marks for his amicable behavior.

Stacy fell silent for a few minutes as they both sat there, feeding the twins. Despite the fact that Cole was actually perched on the edge of the nightstand, it struck her as an incredibly tranquil moment. The kind that every parent looked forward to and relished in the midst of a day filled with small and large chores, surrounded by chaos and organized disorder.

She could get used to this.

"Why do you think she did it?" she asked suddenly, turning toward Cole.

The question came out of the blue and caught him totally off guard. "Who?"

"Their mother." Stacy nodded at the twin in her arms. "Why do you think she abandoned them?" She just couldn't wrap her head around the concept, not after being with them, holding them, taking care of them. "What would make a mother just walk away from her child? Especially *two* of them?"

Cole shrugged. Although he felt the same way, he tried to put himself in the twins' mother's shoes. "Maybe she felt that she couldn't provide for them. It is possible, you know. Or maybe she felt she was too young to be a mother. One night of passion and suddenly, she's faced with this huge responsibility for the next eighteen years. It was too much for her."

He looked at Stacy. "At least she had the presence of mind to leave them on someone's doorstep, in this case, mine. If she'd been completely self-centered, she could have just left them out in the desert."

Stacy shivered, refusing to even go there in her mind. "Don't even say that."

"What I'm saying is that at least she wanted to give the twins a fighting chance. A chance at a decent life."

Stacy pressed her lips together, thinking.

"I'm going to adopt them," Stacy said after a very long pause.

"You're going to *what*?"

"I'm going to adopt them," Stacy repeated very deliberately. "If their mother doesn't turn up—and it's beginning to look like that's highly likely—I'm going to adopt these twins."

That was just her emotions talking, Cole thought. Stacy couldn't possibly know what she was thinking of taking on.

"Stacy…"

She pretended that he wasn't trying to interrupt. He was undoubtedly going to try to shoot her down with logic and she was in no mood to hear it.

Instead, she laid out the plan she'd just come up with. "I have some money that my aunt left me and I can get a job at Olivia's law firm before that runs out. I can be an administrative assistant. And if that doesn't work out, Miss Joan would give me a job. So would Rebecca," she recalled.

His jaw all but dropped open. "You want to be a waitress or a desk clerk?"

It was important to her that she make Cole understand she was serious about this.

"I want to do and be whatever it takes to take care of these little people. They deserve a chance at a life," she insisted. "They deserve to grow up feeling loved, and I do love them."

She looked at Katie and she could feel her heart swelling. This was her purpose. This was what she was meant to do and why she had come home.

"Stacy, you'd be taking on a really huge responsibility." He didn't want to shoot Stacy down, but at the same time, he wanted her to think about what she was getting into.

"I can do it," she assured him without any hesitation.

There was one more point that she was overlooking. "You also need to have a judge approve you adopting the twins," he reminded her. "You're a twenty-five-year-old single woman."

Stacey raised her chin defiantly. The more he argued against it, the more determined she became. "So? Twenty-five-year-old single women have twins," she insisted.

"That they gave birth to. There's a difference if you're trying to adopt them," Cole pointed out. Didn't she see that?

"I'll just have to convince the judge, then." She said that as if it was just a small bump in the road she was going to have to negotiate.

He could see that talking her out of it was out of the question. She had her heart set on this, so he needed to help her.

And himself.

"You'd stand a better chance of adopting them if you were married."

"Yeah, well, I'm not," she said with a toss of her head. "So I'll just have to work harder at convincing the judge—"

"What if you were?"

"What if I were what?" she asked, distracted.

Putting down Mikey's bottle, she placed him against her shoulder and slowly began patting his back, trying to coax a burp out of him so that he would be comfortable.

"What if you were married," he said, wondering if Stacy was paying attention to him at all, or if she was preoccupied trying to find a way to con a judge into letting her adopt the twins.

"Well, I'm *not* married," she reminded him, irritated that he was harping on that point.

Crossing over to her, with Katie against his shoulder, he stood in front of Stacy and asked again, "But what if you could be?"

She stopped patting Mikey's back and looked up at Cole. Confusion gave way to utter surprise as his question sank in.

"Are you asking me to marry you?" she asked in a disbelieving whisper.

"Yes," he said simply, "I am."

"So I can adopt the twins?"

"Well, that would be part of it," Cole admitted, "but—"

"No," Stacy answered firmly. "I can't have you making that sort of a sacrifice. It wouldn't be—"

Damn, but she made it hard to get a word in edgewise. "For once in your life, will you stop talking and let me finish what I have to say?"

Stunned, Stacy stared at him. And then, when she found her voice, she said, "Go ahead."

"I said that you adopting the twins was only part of the reason I'm asking you to marry me. The main reason is because I *want* to marry you. Now that you're finally back and we've cleared up that ridiculous misunderstanding about why you left—which was totally my fault," he quickly interjected lest she went off on another tangent again, "I want to spend the rest of my life with you. I love you, I'm pretty sure you love me and I can't think of any better way to add meaning to my life than to help you raise these twins."

Having said everything that he wanted to say, he paused, waiting for Stacy to answer him.

The pause stretched out, making him feel progressively more uncertain with each second that passed by.

Was she going to turn him down?

Finally, when the silence was close to deafening, Stacy asked, "Are you finished?"

He drew in a breath, bracing himself. She was going to say no. He could see by the expression on her face. But if that was the case, if she was going to turn him down, then he had to face up to it. Better sooner than later.

"Yes," he told her.

"And I can talk now?"

"Yes," he said a little more forcefully.

"Okay, then my answer is—"

Just then, a loud, urgent knock coming from downstairs disrupted everything.

Someone was at the front door.

Chapter Seventeen

The next moment, they could hear Rita responding to whoever was knocking on the door.

"I am coming. I am coming. Have a little patience!" It was more of an order than a request.

Cole exchanged looks with Stacy. Much as he wanted to hear her answer to his question, he could see that her attention had temporarily refocused on the commotion downstairs.

"I'd better go see what's going on," he told Stacy. "I'll be right back."

Stacy felt that she was part of the family now, at least for the time being, and there was no way she was about to just hang back and ignore whoever was knocking on the door so hard.

Maybe she was being paranoid, but she had an uneasy feeling that this wasn't some rancher looking for advice from one of the McCullough brothers.

The knocking had had an ominous sound.

"I'm going with you," she informed Cole before he could leave the room. "Grab a twin," she said, picking up Katie.

Cole frowned. He had not intended to go downstairs to discover what all this noise was about with a baby in his arms. However, since Stacy was obviously coming with him and taking one of the twins, he couldn't very well just leave the other one behind. It didn't seem right.

Scooping Mikey up from the crib, he wound up following Stacy to the stairs.

Apparently, having opened the door and seen who was on the doorstep, Rita had simmered down. Stepping back, she opened the door even wider, allowing Sheriff Rick Santiago to walk into the house.

"Is there something wrong, Sheriff?" Rita asked the man just as Cole and Stacy reached the bottom of the stairs with the twins.

Instead of answering her one way or another, Rick made a request. "I'd like to see Cole or Connor if they're home. Ms. Rowe, too, if she's still staying here."

"Oh, yes, she is still here," Rita assured him as she closed the door again. "She is helping to take care of the babies, you know."

Rick removed his hat. "No, I didn't know. To be honest, I thought she was just helping Cole out with the infants when he stopped at my office."

Rita was not one to waste time with unnecessary dialogue. "You have news?" she asked pointedly.

That was when he saw Stacy and Cole walking into the living room. Each of them was holding an infant.

"I have news," Rick answered, addressing his words to the two younger people rather than to the woman who had let him in.

"What kind of news?" Stacy asked, her voice strained and hollow. She could feel her fingertips instantly turn icy. Her heart racing, she held on to Katie a little tighter. Katie whimpered. Realizing she was gripping the baby too tightly, Stacy loosened her hold a little. She could control that, control her hold. But she couldn't control the way her heart was pounding. If it hammered any harder, it was going to start breaking ribs.

"Is it bad?" Stacy asked, her eyes holding the sheriff's.

Again, he didn't answer the question. Instead, he told them, "Joe Lone Wolf found out who the twins' mother is."

Stacy stopped breathing. She looked at Cole, mutely asking him for help. She couldn't make herself ask the question.

Cole got the message. "Who *is* their mother?" he asked.

Rick gave them the background information first. "For the last six months, the girl was staying with her best friend, Ann Fox Fire. Ann lives with her older sister on the reservation. No one really noticed that the girl was expecting," Rick explained delicately. "I gather that she didn't put on much weight, even though she was carrying twins.

"According to everyone Joe talked to, on the reservation and in town, she really didn't show." Rick paused and then added, "And she worked right here in town."

"Who is it?" Stacy asked impatiently, her nerves getting the better of her. She could just envision the twins' mother being seized with regret and tearfully coming forward, saying it was all a huge mistake and that she wanted her babies back.

"It's Elsie," Rick said.

Stacy stared at the sheriff. "You mean the receptionist from the hotel? The one who was so excited about getting accepted into college that she quit right on the spot?" Stacy asked incredulously.

He had to have made a mistake. It couldn't have been her. Elsie couldn't be the twins' mother. She was practically a baby herself.

"That's the one," Rick told her.

Stacy shook her head. "There has to be some mistake," Stacy told the sheriff. "I was there when she opened her acceptance letter."

"Turns out that was for everyone else's benefit."

Stacy wasn't sure that she understood what he was telling her. "Then she was lying? Elsie wasn't accepted to college?"

"Oh, she was. But she knew about it before she came to work. A full day before, according to Ann." There was no judgment in Rick's voice as he went on to give them the details. "Elsie agonized over the letter and what she was going to do. According to Ann, Elsie felt that finding a really good home for the twins was the best thing she could do for them. And college was the best thing she could do for herself."

Rick looked at Cole. "Your family's getting quite a reputation as being a haven for babies." To drive his point home, Rick elaborated. "Cody wound up taking in not just the baby he helped birth, but the baby's mama, as well. And Cassidy took in that baby she and Will saved from the river."

"So this Elsie decided that it was my turn to get a baby?" Cole asked in disbelief.

"Babies," Rick corrected, nodding at the infants Cole and Stacy were holding. "Yeah, that's about the size of it."

So now she knew who the twins' mother was, Stacy thought, but that still left a lot of questions unanswered—and she was far from at ease.

"Where is Elsie now?" Stacy asked.

"She took off," Rick told her. "Most likely for college. At least, that's what Ann hopes."

That still didn't eliminate possible complications. "What about the twins' father?" Stacy asked. "Doesn't he want them?"

She could just envision giving up her heart to the twins, thinking that they could form a family, only to have their father step out of the shadows and demand custody of the children.

"I really don't think so," Rick said. "According to what Ann said, he was a guest of the hotel for a couple of nights about ten months ago." It was an old, all-too-familiar story. "You know the type, good-looking, sweet-talking. Elsie never stood a chance," Rick concluded, shaking his head. "They spent the night together and then he was gone.

"When she found out she was pregnant, Elsie didn't even know how to get in touch with him. Turns out, the address and phone number that he gave at the hotel when he registered were both fake."

Rita had been standing by quietly all this time, but now broke her silence and shook her head. "That does not surprise me."

Well, they had the parentage straightened out, such as it was, Cole thought.

"So, now what?" he asked the sheriff.

"Now I can get in touch with social services," Rick told them. "It might take a few days, but they'll send someone out to take the twins—"

"No," Stacy cried.

Rick looked at her, surprised by the fierceness of her reaction.

"That's the next logical step," he told her, "since their mother obviously has given up all claim to them and no one knows where their father is."

"No," Stacy insisted. "The next logical step is to make sure that they get a good home."

"That's what I just said," Rick began.

"With me," Stacy stressed.

Rick looked as if he was trying to understand what she was saying. "Let me get this straight. Are you saying you want to be their foster mother?"

"No, Sheriff. What I'm saying is that I want to *adopt* them."

Rick might have been surprised by her declaration, but Rita appeared to take it in stride, as if she had expected this all along.

"They don't need a foster home or to be passed

around from one home to another," Stacy continued. "Or to be separated. What they need is a stable home. They need *me*," she insisted. "And I'll do whatever it takes to keep them."

"And I will help her," Rita said, speaking up authoritatively.

"Stacy," Rick began, "I understand how you feel, but it's not up to me—"

"Elsie obviously wanted to leave them with me," Cole interjected. "She had her pick of places to leave the twins—a lot more accessible places than the side of the bunkhouse at the Healing Ranch," he pointed out to the sheriff. "The fact that she sought me out and left them on what amounted to my doorstep means that she wanted me to look after her twins."

"Go on," Rick said gamely, listening.

"So, in essence," he told the sheriff, "she was asking me to adopt them."

Rick seemed to mull over what Cole had just said. "You have a point."

"And I have the twins," Cole told him. "Possession is still nine-tenths of the law, right?"

"We're not talking about property," Rick pointed out. "We're talking about children—"

"Who are in real danger of getting swallowed up by the system if we turn them over to social services," Stacy insisted. She looked plaintively at Rick and made her appeal. "These kids need a break."

"And you're it?" Rick asked her. Did she realize what she was asking to take on?

"*We're* it," Stacy corrected him, stepping closer to Cole.

"So, you're each going to take one?" Rick questioned uncertainly.

"No," Stacy told him. "I'm going to answer the question that Cole was asking me when you knocked on the door earlier." Turning toward Cole, she smiled up at him and said one word. "Yes."

"You're sure about this?" Cole asked, almost afraid to jump to the conclusion that was shimmering right in front of him.

"Very sure," Stacy answered.

He needed to be sure himself. "You're not just saying yes because—"

She wouldn't let him finish. "I'm saying yes because it's been yes for a long time. And if you hadn't gotten cold feet, you would have known that, you big idiot—"

Cole turned toward the sheriff and said, "Hold on to Mikey for me."

Before he could say anything to Cole, Rick found his arms filled with baby.

Taking Katie from Stacy, Cole turned toward his family housekeeper and told her, "Hold Katie for a minute."

"What are you doing?" Stacy cried.

"A man doesn't just propose to a woman and then go on as if it's business as usual," he told her. "At least, not without sealing the bargain."

"And just how do you intend to do that?" Stacy asked.

"Like this," Cole answered, pulling her to him and kissing her soundly.

"I guess that means that Olivia and I are invited to the wedding?" Rick asked.

Neither party answered, being far too occupied to talk at the moment.

Rick smiled and looked at the baby in his arms. "Looks like you and your sister have got yourselves a brand new mommy and daddy, Mikey," he told the baby.

"Sheriff," Rita said, addressing Rick. "Come with me, please. I have just finished making a pie that you have to try." She began to leave the room, then glanced over her shoulder to make sure the sheriff was following her. "You should know this could go on for a bit. You might as well eat something."

"I like the way you think, Rita," Rick said with a laugh.

Carrying Mikey, he followed the housekeeper out of the room.

Epilogue

The moment she heard that Cole had proposed to Stacy, after announcing a self-satisfied "I knew it!" Miss Joan insisted on throwing the wedding.

"Don't worry, I'm not trying to live out some fantasy," she assured Cole when he protested that it would be too much trouble for her. "I got the wedding of my dreams when Henry came to his senses and finally married me."

Everyone in Forever knew it was actually the other way around and that it was Henry who had finally managed to wear Miss Joan down so that she accepted his proposal, but Cole was not about to be the one to point that out to her.

However, he felt that he did have to make an attempt to protest. "Stacy doesn't want a fuss," he told the woman who had been like a surrogate mother to him.

"Everyone wants a fuss," Miss Joan contradicted him. "But it'll be a small fuss," she promised, patting him on the cheek. "Just right for the occasion. Leave everything up to me. Just give me a date."

"As soon as possible," Cole answered.

He thought that would dissuade her, but he should have known better.

"Perfect," the whiskey-voiced woman said. "I'll call you with the details once I have them. Now shoo." She gestured him out of the diner.

"Careful what you wish for," one of the waitresses murmured to Cole as he walked to the door.

But Cole could only smile. He already had what he wished for. He had Stacy. The fact that he was also going to be the instant father of twins only seemed to make the entire thing that much better.

As far as he was concerned, the wedding ceremony was just an afterthought.

"IT'S BEAUTIFUL," Stacy told Miss Joan as she looked at her reflection in the mirror in the tiny room right off the church vestibule. She was wearing an empire-waisted wedding gown she could have never afforded to buy on her own.

Pleased, Miss Joan smiled. "Just because I wear that old uniform at the diner every day doesn't mean I don't have taste, girl," she told Stacy.

Stacy was afraid she might have insulted Miss Joan. "I didn't mean to imply—"

Miss Joan was quick to assuage her guilt. No harm had been done. "I know, I know. Just get yourself out there and marry that young man. Cole'll be good to you—and to those babies," she told Stacy with unshakable certainty. Miss Joan allowed herself just a hint of a smile as she added, "You all deserve each other."

She looked up as the strains of Mendelssohn's "Wedding March" came floating through the air, reaching the tiny back room of the church. "That's your cue, girl. Time to go out and meet your future."

Stacy turned toward the woman. "Not without you, Miss Joan."

"Excuse me?"

"Walk out with me," Stacy requested. "You can give me away," she told the for-once-speechless older woman. "You put this together for us. That makes you the closest thing I have to family." She paused and then added, "Please?"

Miss Joan sighed. "We'd better go before that old woman gets tired of playing," she mumbled, referring to the church organist.

Stacy threaded her arm through Miss Joan's, and together they came out of the back room and to the back of the church.

Everyone in the church rose in unison. If some were surprised to see Miss Joan leading the bride to the altar, they gave no indication. Everyone had come to expect the unexpected when it came to Miss Joan.

Besides, they were more taken with how beautiful the bride, someone who was, ultimately, one of their own, looked in her bridal gown.

Certainly Cole couldn't take his eyes off her. He could hardly breathe as he watched Stacy slowly walk toward him.

Each of his brothers were holding one of the twins, Mikey, who was dressed in a miniature tux, and Katie, who had on a tiny bridesmaid's dress. As if aware of the special celebration they were part of, both babies were quiet and taking in their surroundings with wide-eyed wonder.

Finally, Stacy reached the front of the church and the man she had been heading toward all of her life.

"Ready?" Cole whispered to her as Miss Joan handed Stacy over.

"More than you could ever possibly know," Stacy answered.

"Then let's get married."

They turned as one to face the minister, ready to say the words that would unite them today and for all eternity.

* * * * *

Don't miss Connor McCullough's story,
A BABY FOR CHRISTMAS
coming December 2017!

And catch up with the rest of the
McCullough siblings:

THE RANCHER AND THE BABY
THE COWBOY AND THE BABY

Available now wherever
Mills & Boon books
and ebooks are sold!

MILLS & BOON®

Cherish™

EXPERIENCE THE ULTIMATE RUSH OF FALLING IN LOVE

A sneak peek at next month's titles...

In stores from 19th October 2017:

- **Newborn Under the Christmas Tree** – Sophie Pembroke *and* **The Rancher's Christmas Song** – RaeAnne Thayne
- **Snowbound with an Heiress** – Jennifer Faye *and* **The Maverick's Snowbound Christmas** – Karen Rose Smith

In stores from 2nd November 2017:

- **Christmas with Her Millionaire Boss** – Barbara Wallace *and* **A Cowboy Family Christmas** – Judy Duarte
- **His Mistletoe Proposal** – Christy McKellen *and* **His by Christmas** – Teresa Southwick

---

Just can't wait?
Buy our books online before they hit the shops!
www.millsandboon.co.uk

Also available as eBooks.

MILLS & BOON®

EXCLUSIVE EXTRACT

Beautiful, young widow Noelle Fryberg is determined to show her Christmas-hating boss, millionaire James Hammond, just how magical Christmas can be…Could she be the one to melt his heart?

Read on for a sneak preview of
CHRISTMAS WITH HER MILLIONAIRE BOSS
the first book in the magical **THE MEN WHO MAKE CHRISTMAS** *duet*

He'd lost his train of thought when she looked up at him, distracted by the sheen left by the snow on her dampened skin. Satiny smooth, it put tempting ideas in his head.

Like kissing her.

"Don't be silly," she replied. For a second, James thought she'd read his mind and meant the kiss, especially after she pulled her arm free from his. "It's a few inches of snow, not the frozen tundra. I think I can handle walking, crowd or no crowd. Now, I don't know about you, but I want my hot cocoa."

She marched toward the end of the aisle, the pom-pom on her hat bobbing in time with her steps. James stood and watched until the crowd threatened to swallow her up before following.

What the hell was wrong with him? Since when did he think about kissing the people he did business with? Worse, Noelle was an employee. Granted, a very attractive, enticing one, but there were a lot of beautiful women working in the Boston office and never once had he contemplated pulling one of them against him and kissing her senseless.

Then again, none of them ever challenged him either. Nor did they walk like the majorette in a fairy band.

It had to be the drone. He'd read that concussions could cause personality changes. Lord knows, he'd been acting out of character for days now starting with agreeing to stay for Thanksgiving.

It certainly explained why he was standing in the middle of this oversized flea market when he could—should—be working. Honestly, did the people in this town ever do anything at a normal scale? Everywhere he looked, someone was pushing Christmas. Holiday sweaters. Gingerbread cookies. One vendor was literally making hand-blown Christmas ornaments on the spot. Further proof he wasn't himself, James almost paused because there was one particularly incandescent blue ornament that was a similar shade to Noelle's eyes.

The lady herself had stopped. At a booth selling scented lotions and soaps wrapped in green and gold cellophane. "Smell this," she said, when he caught up with her. She held an open bottle of skin cream under his nose, and he caught the sweet smell of vanilla. "It's supposed to smell like a Christmas cookie," she said. "What do you think?"

"I like the way your skin smells better."

Don't miss
THE MEN WHO MAKE CHRISTMAS:

CHRISTMAS WITH HER MILLIONAIRE BOSS
by Barbara Wallace
Available November 2017

SNOWED IN WITH THE RELUCTANT TYCOON
by Nina Singh
Available December 2017

www.millsandboon.co.uk

Join Britain's BIGGEST Romance Book Club

- **EXCLUSIVE offers every month**

- **FREE delivery direct to your door**

- **NEVER MISS a title**

- **EARN Bonus Book points**

Call Customer Services
0844 844 1358*

or visit
millsandboon.co.uk/subscription